"*You aren't really looking for a wife, are you?*

You've just stumbled on an ingenious way to score with a broader range of women."

A red flush climbed Joe's neck. "Maybe you're just mad that you aren't one of them."

"Give me a break," Brít said, her eyes narrowing with angry fire. "I'd rather spend the rest of my life in a convent than become another one of your applicants. *I'm* immune to those 'Dillon' eyes."

"Are you?" he asked, his voice rising. "Well, let me tell you something. If you were my type, which you aren't, I could charm you in ten seconds flat, and I wouldn't need an ad in the paper to do it. But since I don't like wasting my time, I'll spare you."

"Thank you so much," she said fiercely, leaning inches from his face to show she wasn't intimidated. "Because trying *would* be a colossal waste of your time."

"Well, we'll just see about that," Joe growled, and before she saw it coming, he took her in his arms and laid claim to her lips.

Dear Reader:

The spirit of the Silhouette Romance Homecoming Celebration lives on as each month we bring you six books by continuing stars!

And we have a galaxy of stars planned for 1988. In the coming months, we're publishing romances by many of your favorite authors such as Annette Broadrick, Sondra Stanford and Brittany Young. Beginning in January, Debbie Macomber has written a trilogy designed to cure any midwinter blues. And that's not all—during the summer, Diana Palmer presents her most engaging heroes and heroines in a trilogy that will be sure to capture your heart.

Your response to these authors and other authors of Silhouette Romances has served as a touchstone for us, and we're pleased to bring you more books with Silhouette's distinctive medley of charm, wit and—above all—romance.

I hope you enjoy this book and the many stories to come. Come home to romance—for always!

Sincerely,

Tara Hughes
Senior Editor
Silhouette Books

TERRI HERRINGTON

Wife
Wanted

Silhouette ❤ *Romance*

Published by Silhouette Books New York

America's Publisher of Contemporary Romance

SILHOUETTE BOOKS
300 E. 42nd St., New York, N.Y. 10017

Copyright © 1988 by Terri Herrington

ISBN: 0-373-08561-3

First Silhouette Books printing February 1988

America's Publisher of Contemporary Romance

Printed in the U.S.A.

Books by Terri Herrington

Silhouette Romance

Blue Fire #318
Lover's Reunion #416
Tangled Triumphs #509
Wife Wanted #561

TERRI HERRINGTON

lives with her supportive husband and daughter in Louisiana, but she has lived in eight states and spent part of her childhood in Holland. She feels that falling in love is the most special feeling in the world, one that she experiences each time she writes or reads a romance.

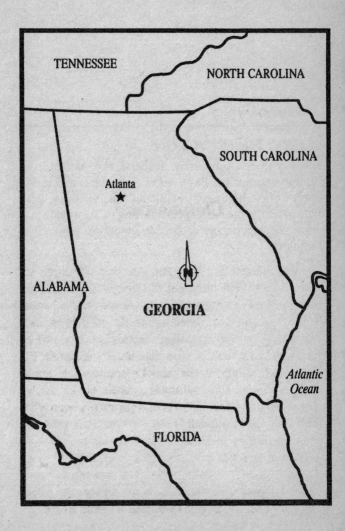

Chapter One

It was incredible, really, Brit Alexander thought as she sat before the hundreds of Georgia Tech students who were obviously anxious to see sparks fly. Leave it to the hotshot, twenty-year-old student union president to turn a college lecture into a point-counterpoint collision. How dare he, in the interest of bigger attendance for the school's lecture series, book her—a woman who had made a career out of teaching women to be happily single—opposite a man who had advertised nationally for a wife? And not just any wife, according to his ad. Preferably a brunette with a college degree (a master's was a plus), a stable family background, fluent knowledge of two or more foreign languages, references, the ability to cook chocolate brownies, and of course, a fertile womb.

And now this wife-seeker—this Joseph Dillon—was actually addressing her with a spark of amusement in his eyes, as if *she* was the unconventional one!

"Why in the world," he asked in his Atlanta shoot-'em-up drawl, "would a woman who looks like you want to go around acting like she doesn't want a man?"

Brit uncrossed her legs and rose higher in her chair. Suddenly the sandy-blond chignon on the back of her head seemed too tight, and her temples rebelled with a dull ache. When was Ted Tarkinton, the too-big-for-his-britches kid who'd come up with this fiasco, going to intervene in his crass way and change the subject, the way he'd done five minutes ago when she'd been on a roll about single women's problems with getting credit?

"Good question," Tarkinton piped in conspiratorially, dashing her hopes of aid.

Brit took a deep, steadying breath. "First of all, Mr. Dillon," she said with a saccharine smile and in her perfectly low-pitched lecture voice, "my looks have nothing to do with my need of a man. Second, I have nothing against men—at least most of them. I just don't happen to feel that I need one in my life. And since there are millions of other women out there who feel the same way, I've made it my business to teach them to have a happy, fulfilled life without the constant pressure for marriage, two-point-five kids and a station wagon."

Joseph Dillon slung an ankle over his knee and stroked his shadowed jaw thoughtfully. A lustrous strand of black hair slid over his forehead, defining the dark, half-shielded eyes beneath it. "I don't buy it," he said simply.

The college audience buzzed with approval, and Brit threw an accusing look at the union president in a vain attempt to solicit his help.

"You don't buy what, Mr. Dillon?" Tarkinton asked with obvious delight.

"The fulfilled-life bit," Dillon said. "I mean, here she is, this good-looking blonde who probably got bored with men falling at her feet before she was twenty years old, swearing off men—"

"I never said I'd sworn off men, Mr. Dillon. And I'm not teaching other women to do that. I just don't happen to need marriage—"

"Uh-huh," he said skeptically, cutting her off again with that deep, sleepy rumble of his. "And what happens one day when Mr. Right charges into your life and sweeps you off your feet? It would sort of ruin your credibility a bit, wouldn't it? Since you've gotten rich trying to make lonely women feel like they don't *need* anyone to love them."

Brit held her breath and tried to stay calm. How could he pack so many punches into one paragraph and look so relaxed at the same time? "Single women are *not* lonely, Mr. Dillon. Most of us are professionals who have chosen to put more energy into our careers than into relationships, just as the young women in this audience may choose to do. And as for Mr. Right charging into my life, that's about as likely as you choosing me for your wife!"

Joseph Dillon seemed to like the idea, judging by the glimmer in his eyes. A devilish grin crept across his face. "Do you have a fluent knowledge of two or more languages?"

"No," she snapped. "I happen to have flunked Spanish. And as for this farce of a marriage you're planning, it should be interesting to see you coming out with a little more humility when you realize after a few months that you can't hire a wife the way you do a secretary!"

"Do I detect a note of hostility toward the way I've gone about my search for a wife?" Dillon asked with enjoyment.

"Do I detect a note of hostility toward the fact that my work could be narrowing down your options a bit?" she returned. "I'd be willing to bet there aren't too many women out there anxious to put themselves on the auction block."

"Try eight thousand," he said smugly.

Brit hesitated. "Eight thousand what?"

"Eight thousand applicants. And I've only had the ad running for a month. Wading through those applications has become a full-time job," he said, "and none of the applicants seem too insulted by my methods. Maybe I could sell you my mailing list when I've made my decision, and you could contact some of these women to teach them how fulfilled and happy they really are without marriage, two-point-five kids and a station wagon."

Ted Tarkinton chose that moment to lean forward, his pimply face curving into that self-satisfied smile of his, and end the confrontation by thanking the guests and asking the audience to return next Wednesday for his new approach to college lectures—when he'd be featuring a male stripper and a Moral Majority leader.

"Wonderful show," Tarkinton said, shaking hands with Brit and Joseph Dillon in turn.

"It wasn't supposed to be a 'show,'" Brit said through clenched teeth. "I've been on the college lecture circuit for a year, and I have *never* been part of a circus like this!"

"Yeah," Dillon threw in with delight. "Wasn't it great?"

As the applause died down and the audience broke up, Tarkinton left the stage to bask in the admiration of his classmates, and Brit glared across the stage at the man who had somehow gotten the best of her. How had he done it?

"So," Joseph Dillon said, unfolding from his chair and rising to his full six feet—six feet of tailored suit, muscle and taunting virility. He rubbed his hands together like a man pleased with himself for a job well-done. "How about we go somewhere for a drink? Get to know each other better?"

Brit managed to steady her legs enough to rise to her feet. Was he serious? After he'd just lambasted her in front of five hundred students, did he really expect to make her forget with that salacious smile and the offer of a drink? "I don't think so," she said as she started off the platform. "We've both said about everything there is to say to each other. And since I'm not in the market for a man, and you *are* in the market for a woman—one whose description I don't happen to fit—it would be a waste of time."

"Oh, come on," he coaxed, following her. "A guy can't be studying applications all the time. Sometimes it's good for the soul to be with someone who doesn't quite measure up. Besides, it'll prove to me that you haven't sworn off men completely."

"Measure up!" A brittle laugh escaped her as she turned back to him. "If you think wanting a brunette who speaks French represents high standards, I feel sorry for you, Mr. Dillon. And furthermore, I don't have to prove to anyone how I feel about men. I happen to have a healthy social life, which includes an occasional date with a man, so you can stop worrying." She gathered her briefcase and purse from a chair beside the door and started to walk away. "Besides, I'm meeting someone."

"Do you always speak in lists?" he asked.

Grudgingly, she turned back again. "What?"

He adopted her stance and mocked her voice. "First of all, second of all, furthermore, besides..."

"Do you always ask a stream of unrelated questions in one breath and expect answers?" she parried, flabbergasted.

His smile started in those obsidian eyes and spread to the corners of his mouth. "Only when I'm trying to see how sharp someone is," he said. "And you're so sharp I suspect I'll be bleeding any minute."

Brit threw a flustered glance to the ceiling. The man could turn Mother Teresa into a raving lunatic. "I'm meeting my…my publicist." There, she thought. That should sound convincing enough.

"Where?" he asked.

"At my hotel, the Waverly," she said before it occurred to her that it was none of his business. "And I'm late, so if you'll excuse me—"

"I'll take you," he said, reaching for the door before she could open it herself. "I noticed you came in a cab. It's the least I can do...."

Brit planted her heels before the threshold, refusing to be bullied. Gritting her teeth, she glared up at him. "Mr. Dillon, you don't owe me anything."

Those thick brows over his eyes formed an apologetic, boyish arch, and he shrugged. "Well, I did just shoot you down in front of an auditorium full of people. I feel sorta bad about it."

"You did not shoot me down!"

"Then why are you so mad at me?"

Brit focused on the floor and tried to regain her composure. She'd had shots fired at her before, and she had always been able to fire back. Why did this particular man leave her angry at herself and so dumbfounded that she couldn't think of an intelligent, scathing response? "I am not mad at you."

"Good, then I'll take you to your hotel. We can have drinks while we wait for your publicist."

Brit closed her eyes and told herself she'd only regret it if she screamed out that *we* weren't going anywhere. Already the lingering members of the audience were stopping to get an earful of the ridiculous exchange, and Ted Tarkinton looked as if he might call the audience back to their seats. Wouldn't it be easier just to accept Dillon's ride and get rid of him afterward than to stand here in front of a twenty-year-old politician with a bad complexion and his gang of cohorts, and come out on the losing end of this verbal sparring match?

When her eyes opened, Dillon was leaning an elbow on the door frame over her shoulder, his appealing gamin grin offering some explanation for why eight thousand women were competing to be his bride. But she wasn't one of them, she reminded herself gratefully.

"You've got to come with me," he whispered with a chuckle. "If you don't, you'll have to stand here with them staring at you for the twenty or thirty minutes it takes to get a cab."

She forced a smile for the benefit of the spectators. "If they're staring at me," she snapped, "it's because you're making a scene."

"It's my style," he acknowledged. "What can I say?" He pointed to the limo idling beside the curb. "The car's that way."

Brit huffed out a defeated breath and asked herself why not. What did she have to lose at this point when she'd already been publicly embarrassed? Besides, she was a unilingual blonde, and Joseph Dillon wanted a trilingual brunette. What could be safer?

Although her rationale seemed sound, in fact, as she started toward the car, she felt about as safe as Horton the Elephant perched on a wavering tree limb. It was a good thing she wasn't easily intimidated by a man's considerable charm. If she were, she would have been running the other way as fast as her high-heeled Guccis would carry her!

Joe shook his head and rubbed his chin as he followed her out of the auditorium, smiling his victory smile and winking mischievously at the students watching nearby. She was cute, all right, he thought as Brit pranced ahead of him. And those lashing blue eyes. Whew! Too bad she was a blonde.

It wasn't that he disliked blondes, really. It was just that there were so few who were genuine. It had been his experience that just when you thought you were holding a real one, you dug deep enough to find out she really had brown roots. So why not save everyone the trouble and order a brunette? he'd decided. That way he'd know what he was getting right up front. But no, he decided as he raked his gaze over Brit Alexander again, he had nothing at all against a real blonde.

Flunked Spanish, huh? he thought with a chuckle. Well, she was a live one. It was refreshing to be around someone ready to bite his head off, instead of someone who was ready to lie down and die while he sampled her brownies. Truth was, this search was getting a little tedious. He needed a distraction like Brit Alexander. Even if it was only for a drink.

Moments later, the limousine chauffeuring them was on its way to the Waverly Hotel, the hulking driver trying and failing to suppress a grin that made Brit remarkably uncomfortable. Joe Dillon was watching her quietly, sitting much too close on the wide seat. Some of her anger at him had dissipated as the intoxicating scent of the sexiest cologne she'd ever encountered filled her senses. It was a tool, she told herself, realizing how lucky she was that she was too smart to fall for it. It would take more than a tantalizing concoction of bomber leather and citrus and man to move her. *Considerably* more! Straightening the bow at the collar of her blouse, she tried to look bored. "Tell the truth. Was that just hype back there, or have you really had eight thousand applicants for that absurd ad of yours?"

"More," he said, sliding down until his head rested on the back of the seat. "I get a bagful every day. It's been much more successful than I expected."

"And what do these women say to you?" she asked, sitting more stiffly the more he relaxed.

He flicked on the radio and began to drum his fingers on the shoe crossed over his knee, keeping time with the rock beat. "Oh, they tell me how well they fit my qualifications, how ready they are to settle down with the 'right' man, how kind my eyes looked in the photo I put in the ad. I worked hard on that picture, you know. Kind is a hard effect to come by." He did a drumroll on his shoe as the song reached a bridge, then resumed his story. "And some send samples of their brownies, which are usually melted or stale beyond belief by the time I open them. And then comes the usual baloney about how their favorite things are making love in the rain, running barefoot in the rain, riding bikes in the rain, picnicking in the rain . . . for some reason, most of these women seem to have an aversion to sunshine."

Against her will, Brit laughed softly.

"There you go," Dillon said, abandoning his drumming. "I knew you could do it."

"Do what?" she asked as her laughter died into a self-conscious smile.

"Crack that frown of yours. I knew there were too many little laugh lines beside those eyes for a woman who only frowned all the time."

"Are you saying my skin is wrinkled?" she asked with mock offense.

"No," he said, lifting a finger and gently stroking the skin beside one powder-blue eye. "I'm saying that those lines have a lot of honesty and character. I don't see much of that these days. Most of the pictures I'm sent are airbrushed." His fingers settled on her cheek, and she swallowed. "So, tell me, why did it take you all this time to start smiling?"

Could he feel the heat scoring her cheeks, or hear the tattoolike pounding of her heart? "You put me on the defensive, Mr. Dillon, and you know it."

"Joe. Call me Joe."

Fighting the smile that came more from a plethora of foreign emotions than from mirth, she closed her hand over his wrist and pulled his hand away from her face. He acknowledged the rebuff with amusement.

"I'll call you Mr. Dillon," she insisted calmly. "You put me on the defensive back there, and I didn't like it. There is absolutely nothing wrong with my teaching single women how to enjoy life, and I thoroughly resented your attacking my motives that way."

"You were the one who called my search for a wife a farce, Brit—it is all right if I call you Brit, isn't it?" He paused long enough for her to object, then went on when she didn't, his hand tugging at his tie as he spoke. "I'd like to know—what is it about my search that offends you so?"

Brit couldn't believe he really didn't know. "You have to admit it isn't exactly a conventional method."

"I tried the conventional methods. They didn't work. All I found were opportunists, gold diggers and shallow little beauties." He slipped off his tie and draped it around her neck. Brit pursed her strengthening grin and pulled the tie off, but Joe didn't seem to notice. "I tried bars until I got tired of playing games, I tried computer services and those bland little getting-to-know-you conversations, I tried taking night classes until I realized that most of the women I met were young enough to be my...little sisters. I finally decided that if I wanted to do this right, I'd take matters into my own hands and start an out-and-out search for a wife." His solemn, determined mien told her he was serious. But why? Why would a man of his obvious financial standing and his blatantly appealing looks want to be tied down with some woman he found by advertising?

"Amazing," she mumbled aloud as the limo pulled to the curb beside her hotel.

He led her into the plush, extravagantly decorated bar, found them a table and seated her with all the savoir faire of Prince Charming at the ball. After they'd ordered two glasses of white wine, Brit settled her blue eyes on his dark face etched with hard-living lines that told her he hadn't always been the husband-father-provider type. Instead, he had more of a raucous facade, a look that screamed lover, a look that denied commitment. "So tell me," she began with a deeply interested frown, "why is it so important to you to find a wife?"

One thick eyebrow arched, and he toyed with the stem of his glass as he pondered his answer. "I turned forty last month," he said, as if that explained everything. "When my father was forty, he had three sons and two grandchildren, and a wife who kept him in line. And I doubt he was lonely a day in his life."

Was that his roundabout way of saying *he* was lonely? Brit wondered, watching the serious cast to his face and asking herself if a man with eyes like his could ever really be lonely. Wasn't it just a restless need he had, a luxury his money hadn't been able to buy, something he wanted to test and would grow tired of when he found it? Couldn't it even be a son's need to follow in his father's footsteps? She fingered her glass, wiping away the condensation. He watched the motion with indolent interest.

"You know," she said quietly, "marriage isn't all it's cracked up to be. My parents divorced after ten years, and they swear it was the best move they ever made. The general consensus seems to be that single people are much happier, much more fulfilled people."

"One, two, three strikes, you're out," he muttered.

"What?"

"My requirements. You're a blonde instead of a brunette, you flunked Spanish, and your parents are divorced." He leaned toward her over the table and pushed a strand of hair out of her eyes. "Too bad you're so darned cute."

Brit turned her head from his touch and mentally kicked herself for grinning like a sixteen-year-old being hit on for the first time. "This may come as a surprise to you, but it doesn't matter to me if I've struck out, since I wasn't aware I was up to bat."

"Well, you weren't really. I don't force myself on people, and until you submit your application, I couldn't really consider you seriously, could I?"

The laughter returned to Brit's eyes, and she wondered why she found this whole idea so amusing, when moments ago it had infuriated her. "The day I apply for the position of your wife and childbearer will be the day they lock me up in a padded room and throw away the key."

Joe hiked his brows and narrowed his eyes seductively. "Don't you think this talk about where we'll spend our honeymoon is a bit premature?" he chuckled.

Brit shook her head, conceding the fact that he was incorrigible, but she found herself leaning closer to him to echo his posture and the intimate tone of his voice. "As a matter of fact, a padded room probably would be an excellent honeymoon suite for you and the poor fool you choose. But you can count me out."

"I told you," he said. "I already have. But we can still be friends, even if you do insist on insulting my bride-to-be."

"I don't know why you'd want to waste your time on someone who isn't on the market."

"Why not?" he asked. "You know, wife-hunting can be a very lonely business."

"I can imagine," Brit said skeptically. Her finger trailed upward to the rim of her glass, and his eyes followed her circular motion with an intensity that made her shiver. "It's probably as grueling as house-hunting or car-hunting. You don't want to take the first thing that comes along, and you never know for sure whether you'll really be able to live with the one you choose. Tell me, are you offering a ninety-day warranty? Any kind of life-back-if-you're-not-satisfied guarantee?"

Her sarcasm didn't seem to offend him. "Don't need any," he said. "I don't intend to make this a trial offer."

Brit set her elbow on the table and propped up her chin as she studied him. He seemed to allow for the fact that people would joke about his search, and that soft sparkle in his eyes—and they *were* kind, if cocky, eyes—when he spoke of it somehow made up for his earlier stabs at her. "Hasn't it occurred to you that probably ninety percent of your applicants are weirdos? And don't you think it's pretty common knowledge that you're the tycoon who owns the largest chain of electronic stores in the United States? I'll bet it isn't just love and commitment most of these women want from you."

"Sure, it's occurred to me," he said. "That's why I asked for references."

Was he really that naive? "What kind of references?" she asked, incredulous. "Ex-husbands, jilted lovers?"

His dark eyes flickered. "You know, I hadn't even thought of that. Might be a good idea. No, I want character references. Bosses, teachers, childhood friends, that sort of thing."

"Don't you think they'd lie to see their girl hooked up with a millionaire?"

He lifted a shoulder nonchalantly. "That's where my impeccable judgment of people comes in." He smiled as if the matter were logically settled.

It was all so simple to him, she thought as a breeze of laughter tickled through her. He didn't even realize it was ludicrous. She studied her drink, trying to put the whole thing into perspective. Maybe he was faking. Maybe it was all a big publicity stunt. Maybe he just wanted national attention, so more people would buy his products. But college lecture tours?

"Speaking of millionaires," he said, cutting into her thoughts, "I hear you're pretty successful." He lifted her hand and regarded the finger that had circled the rim of the glass. Slowly he brought the fingertip to his lips and sucked on the damp tip. "I have this thing about successful women."

Brit's smile faded as a frenetic heat suffused her face. She swallowed and withdrew her hand, but the tingling effect of his wet lips and that tantalizing tongue lingered. She coiled her fingers in her lap and tried to stop shaking, but he wasn't fooled. Her surprise at her own reaction was reflected in his smoky brown eyes. Quickly she lowered her lids and affected a smile—the most jaded smile she could manage, a smile that said, "You're smooth, but I don't ruffle easily." But she knew he saw right through it. She tried to recover her thoughts. What had he been saying? Something about millionaires ... success ... this *thing* he had for women ...

"Well, you can cool off," she said, "because I'm not *that* successful. Mentioning me in the same breath as the word 'millionaire' is a gross distortion."

"But you have made a lot of money."

She shrugged, took a big gulp of wine and tried to look bored, though her heart hadn't yet finished its mad race. "I've done all right. No complaints. I'm working on a deal to do a weekly television show on cable about the problems of single women. It'll be a call-in show—"

"Sort of like Dr. Ruth?" he asked, amused.

"Sort of," she admitted, matching his smile. "And if it works out, I won't have to do quite so much traveling. It wears thin after a while. I have to stay in strange towns for weeks at a time for each seminar and drum up a lot of publicity." She was rambling, she knew, but she couldn't help herself. "In the Atlanta area alone, I have eleven college lectures and seminars for four or more weekends. And these lectures are getting less predictable all the time—"

"Yeah," he cut in, commiserating, "you never know what kind of kook you're going to meet...."

"Exactly." One side of her mouth quirked upward as she watched him drink. Harmless, she reminded herself. He was absolutely harmless. *As long as he doesn't look at you, touch you or talk to you in that maddeningly low voice,* a little devil in her head added. "Tell me," she asked, desperate to keep the subject out of the realm of intimacy, though he seemed bent on getting it there. "Do you do college lectures often, or did you make an exception just to ruin my life?"

He chuckled lightly. "I don't ever do them. I made this exception, not to ruin your life, but because Georgia Tech is my alma mater and they asked me." He surveyed her across his glass, then asked directly, "Speaking of drumming up publicity, where's that publicist you were meeting?"

Brit bit her lip and glanced around while she considered groping for an answer, but there was no use. No one was going to miraculously appear, so she opted for the truth. "I lied."

The admission didn't seem to surprise him in the least. Joseph Dillon merely set his chin in his palm and leaned presumptuously closer. "Now why would you do that to me?" he drawled.

Brit mimicked his position, chin in palm, and met his eyes without wilting, though she'd practically given her heart up for a runaway that would never be caught again. Of course, it was only the wine, she thought. It always did strange things to her. "Because you seemed like a kook and I didn't want to have drinks with you."

"*I* seemed like a kook? Me? You really know how to hurt a guy. Well," he said, as if trying to smooth his own feathers, "I guess the fact that you admitted it means you've changed your mind."

"You're no kook," she said. "Just a little eccentric."

"Just because I want a wife who can whisper to me in a language I can't understand?"

"Make that a lot eccentric," she amended. "And you've intrigued me."

"Have I?" he asked in a bedroom voice. "Have I really?"

"Yes," she said. "I'm fascinated." Her eyes meshed with his a beat too long, and catching herself, she cleared her throat, then qualified her confession. "Fascinated in the way that a scientist would be with a subject."

"Like a trained monkey?" he asked, undaunted.

Brit brought her drink to her lips. "Something like that."

Joe seemed pleased at the analogy that would have insulted another man. "Want to be more fascinated?" His husky timbre sent shivers scampering along her spine. "This trained monkey knows lots of tricks."

Her face burned with the force of white-hot metal. "I don't think so," she said in a shredded voice.

He tipped his head and flicked a stray curl off her cheek. "Come on, I was kidding. I was really talking about my letters. I would think a woman in your line of work would be interested in seeing some of them. You know, like a scientist with a subject. It might lend a new dimension to your teaching."

He had a point, she thought. It would be fascinating to see exactly what these women said to him in their letters. Perhaps it would offer her new insight and help her find a new area that needed to be covered in her seminars. Besides, she really did want to know why eight thousand women would offer themselves up this way.

"You're right," she said finally. "I'd love to see some of them. We could set up an appointment—"

"How about right now? I'm not doing anything, and since you've been stood up by this imaginary publicist of yours, we could mosey on over to my place—"

"Your place?" The words held a note of alarm, and she felt that grin tugging at her lips again. "Oh, no, I don't think so. I thought we'd meet someplace less—"

"Personal?" he provided, settling his chin on his hand again. "Believe me, there are very safe places in my house. For instance, I've rarely attacked women in my study. The kitchen is fairly safe, too. I'd be a little careful in the living room, though, if I were you. But as long as I don't have a fire in the fireplace to set the mood, I'll probably be able to control myself."

Brit wet her lips and struggled against her smile. "I'm not afraid of you."

"I can see that. It's yourself you're afraid of. But who am I to say that's wrong? You probably have good reason."

It was a challenge, and though she knew it, she couldn't deny it. "Let's go," she said, pulling out of her chair.

Joe rose and took her arm, his taunting smile doing crazy things to her stomach. She told herself it was because she'd skipped lunch. "You know," he said as they started out of the bar, "I think I'm going to add a requirement to my list. I want her eyes to be...what do you call that? Azure, indigo, sapphire..."

"You mean blue?" she asked dubiously.

"Whatever," he said as they reached the limousine. He opened the door and helped her step in. "Just as long as it's the color of your eyes."

Brit caught her breath as he closed the door and walked around to his side, where his chauffeur was waiting with his open door. A peculiar grin cut across his rough face, and for a moment Brit considered making a run for it. Maybe she did have something to fear, after all.

Chapter Two

Home, Jerome," Joe drawled to the chauffeur as he settled back on the limo's leather upholstery.

"Yo, Joe," the driver replied in a thick Brooklyn accent that reminded her of Sylvester Stallone. He slid his black hat low over his forehead and gave Brit a quick glance in the rearview mirror when the engine purred to life.

Joe chuckled at Brit's surprised expression. "I tried to find a driver named James," he said, "so I could say, 'Home, James,' but I didn't have any luck."

"So he settled for cheap instead," Jerome threw in. "Course, it was my idea to hire a chauf*feur* in the first place. Since he lost his license and all."

Brit's astonishment slowly changed to amusement, and she glanced over at Joe. "Lost his license?"

"Yeah," Jerome affirmed. "Joe's a lousy driver. The state of Georgia considered him a hazard."

Joe shrugged innocently. "I sorta had a problem with running into things."

"Things?" she asked, growing more amused by the moment. "What kind of things?"

Before Joe could answer, Jerome slid his hat back and said, "You know. Garbage cans, mailboxes, telephone poles, an occasional fender. Knocked down a power pole once and all of Marietta had to do without electricity for five hours...."

"I had a lot on my mind that day," Joe piped in indignantly. "I'm a busy man. Besides, I never hit a person."

"Just a matter of time," Jerome commented, waving him off and glancing at Brit again. "So he hired me to drive him around till he could find a wife."

Brit tried to suppress her astounded giggle. "Another requirement? She has to have a good driving record?"

"Yeah, well, that goes without saying," Joe muttered.

"I see." She smiled at the man in the front seat. "And what will happen to Jerome then?"

"Jerome's an actor. He's trying to do regional theater here. Figures by the time I narrow down my choices, he'll have been discovered."

"Yeah," Jerome added. "I'm right on the verge. I'm doing Hamlet right now—title role—and as soon as the right producer happens in...I'm outa here."

"Hamlet?" She struggled to keep from laughing aloud. In her mind she heard Hamlet's soliloquy in thick Brooklyn English. *To be, uh not to be. Oh-ay, now dere's de question.*

Somehow Jerome's presence made Joe's effect on her a bit easier to bear. She wished he'd been so relaxed earlier when she'd been full of apprehensions about accepting Joe's ride. "Jerome, why didn't you say anything on the way over to my hotel?" she asked. "I thought you were..."

"A real chauffeur?" he asked. "Hey, what can I say? I'm a ta-rrific actor."

"And I paid him extra to keep his mouth shut long enough for me to impress you," Joe added. "We both figure by now I've got you wrapped around my finger."

Despite her instinct not to, Brit laughed again, shaking her head in disbelief at Joe's cocky self-confidence. The bantering continued as they drove out of Atlanta, through the suburb of Marietta, to the outskirts where only a few houses sprinkled the landscape every few miles. Brit watched in the distance, expecting to see a Tudor castle stretching up into the clouds, a sign of his enormous wealth and fairy-tale standards. So when they pulled onto a gravel road that led to the modest-sized house that was a combination of log cabin and Victorian detail, she caught her breath.

"*This* is where you live? A log cabin?"

"Beautiful, huh?" Joe said, eyes twinkling as he beheld the rustic structure.

"Yes, it is. I just expected some mansion or some-thing...."

"You can't raise kids in a mansion," he said, look-ing at her as if she'd just stepped off the bus from Po-dunk. "They need warmth and light and a house that's small enough that they all wind up in the same room a lot. And lots of room to run and play outside...."

She noted the glimmer in his eyes as he spoke of it, the distant focus, as if he could see it. A fleeting hint of admiration ribboned through her. "You have kids?" she asked.

The question shook him out of his reverie. "Of course not. Not until I get married. But then..."

A foreign sensation took hold of her at his dreamy assessment of what a home should be. Her heart twisted for a moment, and from some recess deep within, she almost hoped he would get what he wanted.

The house, though made of logs, possessed a com-bination of elegance and intimacy that welcomed im-mediately. With its twenty-two-foot-high ceiling in the den and the handmade wall hangings and the colorful rugs thrown about on the hardwood floor, it was like no other bachelor's home she'd ever seen. It was dec-orated for a family, with the mini-tables set in the corners and the pillow-covered seats in front of the bay windows. A loft held the upstairs bedrooms, and through the open doors she could see frilly curtains in one room and more masculine checkered ones in the other, as if the rooms were already occupied.

"You like it?" he asked, hope in his dark eyes.

"It's lovely," she whispered.

"I hired a special team of architects to help me design it," he said. "It's bigger than it looks. Through that little hall between the upstairs rooms, you can reach two more bedrooms. The master bedroom is down here. Come on, I'll show you."

"Uh . . ." Brit held back, knowing she was getting in over her head. "I don't think so, Joe. Maybe we should get right to those applications."

He smirked and assessed her mirthfully. "Okay, but don't expect me to look at *your* bedroom when I visit you if you won't even look at mine."

Again, her lips crescented upward against her will. "I think I can safely agree to that."

"All right," he said with a defeated sigh. "Let's get down to the nitty-gritty. It's teach-Brit-a-lesson-about-women's-deepest-desires time."

With no further ado, he led Brit into a large, rustic study where envelopes were piled four feet deep on the floor, photographs of sexy brunettes draped the walls and boxes of stale brownies graced one long table. On his desk sat a computer, its green lettering filling the screen.

"This is a joke, right?" Brit asked suspiciously, laughter lacing her voice. "These aren't all from women who want to be your wife, are they?"

"Jerome picked up another batch today," Joe said wearily. "It's still in the car." He pointed to one of the stacks on the floor. "Those are the ones I've narrowed it down to so far. I'm in the process of getting the most promising ones on computer. I had to hire someone to do that from my office downtown, but it'll make it easier to narrow it down.''

"Computer! You're letting a computer choose your wife?''

"No, of course not,'' he said, indignant. "I still read every one that comes in. But it isn't easy. The computer adds a little order to it.'' He lifted an envelope from the "unopened" stack and tore into it. "Look at this,'' he said, pulling out the application. He grimaced at the melted, flattened brownies in a Ziploc bag and tossed them into the trash. "Oh, no,'' he groaned when he reached in again. "Another pair of panties. What am I gonna do with all these panties?''

"Panties! These women send you panties?'' she sputtered.

"Yeah,'' he said, rolling his eyes. "And just between you and me, babe, I wouldn't mind if your seminars did reach a few of these. Anybody who'd send a pair of panties through the mail...'' His voice trailed off as he pulled out an eight-by-ten glossy. "On the other hand...'' he began, a leering smile creeping across his face.

Brit grabbed the photo and saw a full-bosomed beauty with luscious black hair trailing down her bare back. Her face was turned to the camera, her eyes were heavy-lidded, and her lips were puckered in a seductive kiss. One hand brushed lazily through roots that Brit was certain had been dyed to meet the requirements. "Really, Joe. You want a woman like this having your babies?''

"The preliminary work might not be too bad," he said, still grinning. He took back the picture, went to his bulletin board and thumbtacked it between what looked to Brit like a hopeless hussy in a bikini and a stripper about to take it all off.

"That's so typical of a man," she said, disgusted.

"What is?" he asked, standing back to survey the photo again.

"Having a decent, if naive, objective and letting it get clouded with a full bosom and a pair of puckered lips!"

"I didn't put her on the computer list, did I?" he asked. "I just hung her up to look at!"

"Well, if you're so all-fired sure you're ready to settle down into family life, what are you doing with a bunch of half-naked women hanging all over your study?"

"Hey, don't treat me like some kind of lech. You don't see my collection of panties anywhere, do you?"

"You probably lined your bedroom walls with them," she returned.

That incorrigible grin lit his face again. "Well, if I recall, you had the chance to find out a minute ago."

"Thanks, but no thanks," she said, crossing her arms obstinately. "I don't even know why I came here."

"Because you wanted to read some of the applications," he said. He cleared some letters off a chair and gestured for her to sit down. "Go ahead. Start reading. I'll get you a couple of brownies and something to drink."

Brit lowered herself stiffly into the chair and watched him rummage through the flattened, hardened brownies. "I don't want a brownie," she snapped. "Could we just get on with this?"

"What are you so ticked off about?"

"I'm ticked off because I happen to be a women's advocate trying to teach women to have more self-respect than to use their bodies or brownies to get a man. It makes me mad."

Insulted, he glared at her. "You think I'd pick a wife on the basis of her body or her brownies?"

"Of course you would. Why else would you have them plastered all over this place?"

The hint of a smile tugged at his lips. "Decoration," he said. "I haven't had time to decorate this room yet."

Piqued at the ridiculous explanation, Brit jerked an envelope from a pile and viciously tore it open. "You don't want a wife, Joe Dillon, you want an incubator to fill up those little fantasy bedrooms you have upstairs, and a warm body to roll with at night, and a driver and cook, and a nice little decoration to perch on your couch."

"I resent that!" he said.

"So do I!" she volleyed. Digging into the envelope, she jerked out the photo and saw that this one, while pretty, was clad in more decent clothes. "Well, give her credit for some intelligence," she said angrily. "She didn't send any godforsaken brownies. Says she knew they wouldn't be good by the time they got here, but she offers to bake them 'personally,' anytime you say." She sent the photo flying, Frisbee-style, across the room to him. "Sign her up, Joe. She works as a translator for the state department. Says she speaks not two foreign languages, but three! She'll give it all up for you, though." She shook the paper, as if it were the woman herself. "I can't believe this! It's got to be a lie. No one in her right mind would—"

"Let me see that," Joe cut in hopefully, stepping over the piles to grab the application. A serious glint sharpened his eyes as he scanned it. "Perfect," he whispered. He went to the chair behind the computer and started entering the information.

Barely harnessing the fury choking her, Brit seized another envelope. She tore into it and drew out a G-string. "I want your mailing list!" she shouted, flinging it across the room. It landed on Joe's head, provoking a broad grin. "I have *got* to shake some sense into these women!"

She threw down that envelope, afraid to pull out the picture of a woman who wore G-strings, and grabbed another, her heart pounding in rage. "Oh, good," she shouted loudly enough to wake snoozers in the next county. "This one comes from a family of twelve! Says her womb's just waiting to be fertilized! Oh, and look! Here she is dressed in the Dutch national costume!" She flung the picture across the room. "Her eyebrows are red, Joe! Red! Do you think a *real* brunette would have *red* eyebrows?"

Joe began to laugh, just a little at first, but by the time he'd left the computer and walked around the desk, he was giving in to full-fledged howls.

"It isn't funny!" she rasped. "It's ludicrous!"

"You're so upset," he said when he caught his breath. "You're taking this personally."

"I am not! It's just so incredible...."

"Yes, you are." His laughter died off a little, only to erupt again in tiny chuckles as he wiped at his moist eyes. "How can a women's advocate, as you call yourself, have so much contempt for women?"

"I do not have contempt for women! Just the ones who—"

"Just the ones who don't follow all of your beliefs," he said. "The ones who go by their own set of rules."

"Rules! These women don't have rules! They're willing to sell themselves like a side of beef for a man they've never even met!"

"Life is a gamble for some people," he said, his eyes sobering slowly. "I don't want the woman I marry to be afraid of taking chances."

"Taking chances is one thing. Jumping into a marriage with a stranger is another."

"They won't be jumping into marriage, and neither will I. I don't plan to make my final choice until I've spent some time with some of them."

"You mean sampled them, like brownies?"

He laughed again. "You really are taking this personally. Your face is red."

Brit sprang up and faced him squarely, fists perched on her hips. "I can just see you returning these panties personally to the senders. Like Prince Charming, you'll search for the one who fits into your favorite pair. Tell the truth, Joe. You aren't really looking for a wife, are you? You've just stumbled on an ingenious way to score with a broader range of women, haven't you?"

A red flush climbed his neck. "Maybe you're just mad that you aren't one of them."

"Give me a break," she said, eyes narrowing with angry fire. "I'd rather spend the rest of my life in a convent than become another one of your bimbo applicants. *I'm* immune to those 'kind' Dillon eyes."

"Are you?" he asked, his voice rising. "Well, let me tell you something. If you were my type, which you aren't, I could charm you in ten seconds flat, and I wouldn't need an ad in the paper to do it. But since I don't like wasting my time, I'll spare you."

"Thank you so much," she said fiercely, leaning inches from his face to show she wasn't intimidated. "Because trying *would* be a colossal waste of your time."

"You think so?"

"I know so!"

"Well, we'll just see about that!" he said, and before she saw it coming, he took her in his arms and laid claim to her lips. She squirmed and squealed against his mouth as he pried her lips open. A soft, velvety tongue slipped inside to flirt with hers unmercifully, and she warned herself that if she gave any sign of softening, she'd make herself shave her head and cut up all of her credit cards. She fought harder. He tasted of lime Life Savers, and smelled like a clean shirt. She forced herself to imagine the taste of castor oil and mentally chanted the words to "Dead Skunk in the Middle of the Road." She fought harder, this time breaking free.

"Call me a cab!" she cried breathlessly.

He stumbled back, running a hand through his hair. "God, I'm sorry," he rasped. "You know how to bring out the worst in a guy, don't you?"

"Me?" she shouted, her words quivering on her heaving breath. "You've been at this game for so long, you think every woman you touch is yours." She scooped up a handful of applications and spread them like cards. "Pick a girl, any girl!"

"Brit—"

"Call me a cab!" she demanded again, throwing the applications in the air, only to have them flutter back down around her. "I mean it. If you don't, I'll walk."

"Damn, you have a rotten temper!"

"Fine," she said, stepping over the stacks. "I'll walk, then."

"I'll get Jerome!" he shouted belligerently.

He went after the driver, and not willing to spend one more moment under his roof, Brit waited on the front porch, pacing rapidly back and forth. In a moment, the car came around with Joe riding in the passenger seat. He got out wearily, genuine regret in those midnight eyes.

"Brit, I really am sorry. I don't usually...I *never* act like that. Really."

"Save it for somebody who matters," she said getting into the car when he opened the back door for her.

"But I don't want you to think I'm some kind of a—"

"I have a very clear picture of you," she cut in. "You don't have to worry about my getting the wrong idea. I'm a fast learner."

"Aw, hell." Joe slammed the door.

Brit watched out the window as he waved her off the way he would a pestering fly and huffed back into the house.

"He ain't so bad," Jerome finally ventured after they'd traveled for miles in silence. "Joe's under a lot of pressure."

"He thinks he's God's gift to the female of the species," she said.

"Well, there are a good many females who think so."

"I don't happen to be one of them."

"Yeah, I kinda got that impression."

Silence stretched between them for a few more miles before Jerome tried again. "He's a good guy, ol' Joe. Best friend a guy could have. Just gets a little mixed up sometimes. He's spent his whole life following in his dad's footsteps, and now he figures he's left out the most important part. At least, that's how he explained it to me."

"Other men have methods a bit more...tolerable," she said.

"Maybe so. But other men ain't Joe. He's been burned, you know. Gals he cared about who were only interested in his money. Guess he just thinks he hasn't got anything to lose by opening the field for someone he can handpick."

Handpick! It was so infuriating it made her want to break something. She ground her teeth and searched for a change of subject before her blood pressure did any damage. "Tell me, Jerome. How did you meet Joe?"

"When he was in New York, 'bout to marry Diana," Jerome said.

"Diana? You mean he almost married once?"

Jerome nodded. "You got it."

A knot tightened in Brit's stomach, and she forced herself not to ask him to expound. Apparently the marriage had been called off. What did she care that Joe had been in love with some wimp named Diana? He'd probably broken the engagement when she came clean and admitted she spoke only English. Brit tried to look interested in the sights out her window.

"Joe got wise just before they could tie the knot, though," Jerome added. "Overheard her bragging about how rich she was gonna be as his wife and decided he wasn't gonna be her free ride. I was working for a florist and tried to deliver her some flowers he'd sent, but he headed me off, got back in the van with me and told me to take him to the airport. We kind of struck up a friendship after that."

The disheartening picture of a disillusioned Joe softened her anger, but she wanted desperately to cling to it. He deserved to be hurt, she thought meekly. Anyone with expectations like his was doomed to fail. It didn't matter to her at all. "So is he the reason you came here?"

"Naw," Jerome said. "I came to act. Everybody thinks New York's the place to be to get started in acting, but they're wrong. Too much competition, you know, not enough parts. Atlanta's turning into a new center for that kind of thing, so I came down here. It's been great. I've had one part after another...."

Brit's mind wandered back to Joe Dillon, with his flat black brows arched upward in pain the way they had been when he'd tried to apologize. Was that how he'd looked when he overheard that Diana person admitting to her reason for marrying him? So much for his impeccable judgment of people.

"Tell the truth, Jerome," she said quietly, interrupting his chatter about his acting career. "Is Joe really looking for a wife? Or is this some kind of gimmick?"

"What do you mean, a gimmick?" Jerome seemed insulted.

"You know. A publicity stunt for his products, a big hoax, a way to have women fall at his feet? Even revenge on that Diana person. A gimmick."

"That's not Joe's style," he said with a hint of irritation in his thick voice. "Joe don't need gimmicks. The man's getting married. And if I know Joe, he'll get a hell of a wife and a whole crew of little kiddies to fill up his house. And he won't care a whole lot whether you thought he could do it.''

Brit only stared out the limo's window, feeling a little like a rebel who'd just insulted some sacred king-figure in front of his most loyal and volatile subject.

Chapter Three

The message in Brit's hand seemed almost alive as she read it for the thousandth time. "Mr. Halbrook from WTBS wants to meet you for breakfast at nine tomorrow. Call his secretary to confirm."

Brit paced the length of her hotel suite, practicing the breathing techniques she used when butterflies threatened her before a lecture. She had been expecting the television producer to call. Her agent had kept her abreast of her progress in making the deal for her syndicated television show, but it was such a big dream that Brit had almost expected it to fall through. Now he wanted to meet her to discuss possible formats for the call-in show, and she was a nervous wreck. She'd have to make a good impression, but what if she stumbled going into the restaurant, or choked on her food? What if she spilled her orange juice all over the producer's nine-hundred-dollar suit?

Oh, Lord, she thought, rushing into the bathroom to start her bathwater. She'd soak until the butterflies drowned, and then she'd calmly prepare what she was going to say. She was ready for this. After all, she'd worked for months on her proposal for this show.

She went to the mirror and began pulling out the pins in her hair, letting the thick, straw-colored strands fall to her shoulders. Her record spoke for itself. She'd had phenomenal success with her seminars, and her lecture tour was reaching hundreds more. . . .

Her hand froze in her hair as she recalled the fiasco at the college campus earlier in the day. Was it possible Mr. Halbrook had heard about how the infamous Joseph Dillon had roasted her in front of the Georgia Tech student body? What if he found out between now and tomorrow morning? Surely a man about to sink a hunk of money into a weekly television show would have had her checked out when she was speaking in his own town. If he didn't know already, it was just a matter of time.

She dropped her hands and leaned over the sink, peering into the mirror as the steam from the hot water began to fill the air. She hadn't handled herself very well today. Not well at all. She'd let Joe get to her on stage, and then she'd practically had what her mother would have called a "hissy fit" when she started reading his applications. He'd been right; she did have a horrible temper. But he had been so incorrigible, so arrogant, so. . . disarming. That was it, she thought.

What really made her angry was that he had disarmed her, whether she'd let him know it or not. He had bullied her into his arms and kissed her like a man possessed, and she'd had to fight *herself* more than him.

She let out a long, irritated sigh and began undressing. She stepped out of her dress, rubbed the mirror clear, and surveyed the lace teddy she wore beneath it. It was too much like one that one of Joe's "applicants" had worn in a photograph he'd had in an honored place on his wall. The white lace had dipped over full breasts, much fuller than Brit's, and formed over a tiny waist and the longest legs she'd ever seen. Brit set a foot on the toilet seat and leaned into her knee, lifting a shoulder the way the woman in the picture had done, and leered at herself in the mirror.

The sound of running water shook her out of her reverie, and she turned it off, then peeled off the teddy. Before stepping into the hot water, she turned her bare back to the mirror and looked at herself over her shoulder, puckering her lips the way the siren with the obscene panties had done in her picture. Her hair fell provocatively over her face, and she tossed it back with a flick of her head.

Still in character, she slunk across the floor, then stepped into the hot water. She kept that heavy, daring look in her eyes as she lowered herself into the tub. She wiped the steam off the chrome faucet with her foot and caught her reflection. She looked ridiculous, she thought. She was *being* ridiculous. The last thing she wanted was to look like one of his bimbos. Besides, she was a blonde, and he . . . well, he was a jerk.

Humiliated that he'd started her thinking like an adoring fan or an aspiring sexpot, she slid down into the water, letting it bury her head and erase the silly image once and for all.

The image of brunette perfection gazed out at Joe Dillon from the glossy eight-by-ten, but he wasn't fazed, for he'd seen at least fifty that day, all just as brunette and just as perfect.

Frustrated, he sent the picture sailing across the room, rubbed his eyes and tried once again to find something *different* about her application. But as far as he could tell, she was just like all the others.

Pick a girl, any girl. Brit had been so angry when she'd shouted that at him. But she didn't understand that he wasn't blindly picking the first acceptable applicant to come along. He was looking for something special. Someone who could hold his attention for the rest of his life. He was just going about it systematically.

He leaned back in his high-backed leather chair and closed his eyes, listening to the mocking silence that almost hurt his ears. The orchestra of his imagination filled the quiet with a symphony of voices, the pitter-patter of little feet and laughter that echoed through the loneliness. It would happen. He would *make* it happen. And all the Brit Alexanders in the world wouldn't stop him.

He opened his eyes and leaned forward to punch up a list of the narrowed-down choices on his computer. Pulling out a box from under his desk, he checked each photograph against the statistics he had on them. Most of these were fully dressed, smiling wholesome smiles, and borderline to right-over-the-top knock-outs. None of them moved him.

You're getting jaded, he told himself. *They're all beginning to look alike.* It was personalities he needed. Real, live, effervescent, intelligent, self-respecting personalities. And tempers, instead of this falling-at-his-feet adoration. And disinterest—like that Brit Alexander had shown him.

Forcing his thoughts away from the maddening woman, he picked up another unopened envelope, lashing himself mentally while he pried off the staples. He should never have pulled the macho act and kissed her. That was stupid. It only proved her theory—whatever it was—about him. And it made him look like an egomaniac. He didn't blame her, really, for being mad about the panties and provocative pictures. And he certainly didn't blame her for being mad about his me-Tarzan-you-Jane act. What he blamed her for was getting under his skin and making his task here harder than it had to be.

He pulled out the smashed brownies, the stained application, the sordid picture, and jumped when something hard fell out into his lap. Something pink and molded...something... He lifted it between thumb and finger, frowning at the object that looked like the imprint of a set of teeth! It couldn't be, and yet . . .

He sifted through the pages of the letter he held and found the notation about the mold. "I've been told I have great teeth," she wrote. "Thought you might want to see for yourself. Our children will have beautiful smiles."

Joe dropped the pink mold onto his desk as if it would infect his hand, then scooted back and stared at it from a distance. A slow grin captured his frown, melted it and skittered across his face. A mold of her teeth? His shoulders began to shake with ready-for-the-loony-farm laughter, Oh, God. Brit *had* to see this! She just had to.

Tears filled his eyes, and he rubbed at them as he leaned back and let his laughter howl to the ceiling. It filled the house, echoed from the walls and came back to him.

But there was no one there to laugh with him.

Brit hobbled in one blue shoe across the plush hotel suite the next morning while she rolled one long strand of hair into a hot roller, clipped it on her head and reached for another one in the pocket of her robe. She'd spent entirely too much time putting on her makeup, she told herself. Her hair would take at least fifteen minutes to set, she needed to iron her dress, and she couldn't find her other shoe!

Why had she agreed to let Mr. Halbrook meet her here? Why hadn't she just told him to meet her in the lobby, where things were more orderly and he wouldn't see the havoc his meeting had wreaked on her? Clipping the roller into her hair, she dug through her unpacked suitcase for that other shoe. Still it eluded her.

She rushed back to the bathroom, piled more hot rollers into her pocket, then plugged in her iron. She'd never be ready on time! He'd probably show up early and see her standing here in one shoe with rollers in her hair, and her whole career would be down the drain.

Hobbling to the bed, she got down on her knees to look for her shoe underneath it. A strand of hair fell into her face and she remembered that she hadn't finished rolling it. Sitting back on her heels, she grabbed a roller out of her pocket and started to wrap another strand of hair around it.

Suddenly a knock sounded on the door, and she dropped the roller. She watched, horrified, as it went rolling across the floor. Oh Lord, she thought, panicked. Her clock was wrong. Either that or Halbrook was one of those insufferable ogres who shows up everywhere early. What was she going to do?

The knock came again, and she contemplated answering the door and swearing she was Brit's twin sister. She'd tell him Brit was downstairs in the lobby. Then when she got rid of him, she could throw her wrinkled dress on, unroll her hair and try to beat him down....

The knock became more urgent, and Brit hobbled to the door, forgetting the one high-heeled shoe she wore. She stared at the door miserably. "Yes?" she asked in a cracked voice.

"Brit?"

The voice didn't sound like the man she had pictured—balding, a little on the heavy side, dominatingly gruff. "Yes?" she asked weakly.

"It's me, Joe."

Brit collapsed against the door in relief and pulled it open. "Thank heaven..." she breathed as he came in.

An amused smile pulled at his lips as he looked down and saw her standing lopsided in that one shoe, with that terry-cloth robe wrapped around her and half of her hair in rollers.

Forgetting her anger at him the day before, she began pulling rollers out of her pockets and wrapping her hair again. "Don't just stand there laughing at me," she said frantically. "Find my shoe!"

Joe bit back his urge to laugh, for he could see he had caught her in a vulnerable emergency state—his favorite way to catch a woman. "I assume it looks just like that one?" he asked, pointing to the one shoe she wore.

"Brilliant." She grabbed her dress off a hanger and rushed into the bathroom. "Hotel rooms never have enough sockets," she railed. "How do they expect a person to iron her dress if the cord won't reach?"

Joe found her shoe inside her garment bag and pulled it out. "Are you getting ready to go somewhere?" he asked.

"Genius," she muttered, remembering that her hair still wasn't finished. "Oh, no, my rollers are getting cold, and I haven't finished—"

"I'll iron the dress," Joe said, slipping into the bathroom behind her and unplugging the iron. "I'll do it on the bed out here, and you finish your hair. Oh, and here's your shoe."

He bent down and slid it onto her foot, giving her immediate balance and poise. His hand lingered on her small ankle for a moment, and his eyes swept the length of her long leg, then on up her robed body to settle on her eyes. Brit froze, her hands in her hair, and looked down at him as if seeing him for the first time this morning. "Thank you," she whispered.

"No problem." He let go and stood up, grabbed her dress and rushed to the outlet near the bed. "So, where are you going in such a frenzy?"

"A business meeting," she said, noticing that her hands were suddenly shaking. Good Lord, she looked awful in this robe. Why hadn't she brought the pink satin one her mother had given her for Christmas? "A producer, about my television show."

"Is he coming here?"

"Yes, heaven help me."

"Well, I don't know about heaven," Joe said, "but Uncle Joe's here. I'll be glad to help."

Brit stared at him for a moment, torn between following her better judgment to get rid of him while she could and the practical urge to put him to good use. But there was no time for weighing one consequence against another. Besides, he'd already started ironing her dress.

When her hair was rolled, Brit came out of the bathroom, trying to look a bit more graceful in the worn, frayed robe. Joe smiled as if the whole situation delighted him and handed her the freshly pressed dress. "Thanks," she said again.

"You probably want the room to be a little neater, huh?"

"Well...yes. But you don't...I mean...I don't even know why you're here."

"Go get dressed," he ordered. "I'll tell you while I straighten up. Good grief, how do you ever make your appointments without help?"

Brit smirked at the last remark, then withdrew to the bathroom to slip into her dress. She closed the door and pulled off her robe. "Really, Joe. Why are you here?"

"To try to apologize again," he called. "I figured if I caught you first thing in the morning, you might not be quite so ornery."

"I wasn't ornery yesterday. I was appalled."

"Well, yeah," he called. "I guess I didn't help matters."

"Not really," she admitted. She slipped on her dress, zipped it up, then sifted through her jewelry bag for the right accessories.

"Do you forgive me?"

"I don't know," she hedged.

"Come on, Brit. I've made up your bed and everything."

Looking at herself in the mirror, Brit caught the unmistakable smile twinkling in her eyes. "Okay," she said quietly. "You caught me at a bad time. I'm weak this morning. I don't have time to fight with you."

She began taking down her rollers, hoping she'd given them enough time to do their job. Whether they had or not, she had no intention of letting Joe see her in that frazzled state again. Full curls tumbled out, and she pulled a brush through the bouncy waves.

"I also came to make you a proposition."

"I won't marry you, Joe."

Joe laughed aloud, and she could hear him coming closer to the bathroom door. "Not that," he said. "I told you, you don't meet the requirements."

Requirements! Why did that word grate on her nerves? she wondered. After all, it had nothing to do with her. Chagrined, she began to tidy up the bathroom, hanging towels over the bar and wiping the residual water from the sink. Her heart pattered unreasonably in her chest, and she couldn't make herself open that door until it had slowed.

"This is a business proposition," he went on through the door. "A very lucrative one."

Curiosity piqued, Brit opened the door and saw him leaning, indolently sexy, against the doorjamb. "What kind of business?" she asked reluctantly. Had his eyes been that black yesterday, or as clear as they were today?

"I need someone to help me with my applications," he said. God, her hair looked gorgeous all curled around her shoulders like that. He cleared his throat. "Someone objective to help me narrow them down. They're all starting to look alike to me, you know."

"They *are* all alike, Joe. Your requirements were pretty specific."

"Well, will you help me? As a friend?"

"I don't think so." Brit pushed past him and walked across the surprisingly neat room, wondering how he'd managed to straighten it so quickly. She'd probably never be able to find anything when she got back, but she wasn't complaining. "High blood pressure runs in my family, and so far I've been able to avoid it. That kind of stimulus might just do me in."

"You seem like you could use a few laughs," he said. "Believe me, you'll find a lot of them in those stacks."

"I don't find that kind of thing funny," she said. She checked the clock. She still had fifteen minutes, but she'd have to get rid of Joe before Halbrook got here.

"Maybe not panties and brownies," he said, "but how about teeth?"

Brit turned around, regarding him with incipient laughter in her eyes. "You're kidding, right?"

"Well, not teeth *exactly*. Sort of a mold. This." He pulled the wrapped mold out of his pocket, peeled off the tissue paper he'd wrapped it in, and brandished it for her.

Brit's mouth fell open. "Someone sent you a mold of her teeth?"

He chuckled. "Yeah. Guess she figured that you don't buy a horse without checking its teeth, so..."

"That's disgusting," Brit said, but the amusement on her twitching mouth belied her words. She began to laugh, and the sound hushed the echoing quiet in Joe's soul. He stood up and joined her, smiling down as she gave in to gales of laughter.

"See?" he asked. "Sometimes it can be fun opening these. You never know what you'll find next."

Her laughter diminished slowly, and finally she sighed. "Yeah, who knows? Maybe one day you'll even find a wife." The thought sobered her too quickly, and she turned away from him and began looking through her purse for her room key. "I really don't want any part of it, Joe. And I hate to be rude after you helped me get ready and everything, but I really would rather you weren't here when Mr. Halbrook comes. He might think—"

"What if I give you the rights?" he asked, casting off the polite dismissal. "The rights to the letters."

"Rights? What would I want with the rights?"

"You could write a book when I'm finished. Surely there's a pattern there that would interest a women's advocate. A lesson to be learned. Something the public would be interested in. There must be, or I wouldn't be getting so much publicity."

She stopped trying to occupy her shaky hands and looked at him fully. "I...I don't know, Joe. I'm not a writer. And I really don't think those letters represent the average woman of the eighties."

"Just think about it," he said. "Maybe you need to look at some more. Whether you write the book or not, I need your help. The letters are fascinating, Brit, and they're bound to be of some use to you. Even if only to reinforce your own beliefs."

Brit glanced at the clock again. It was getting late, and she needed a minute to look over her notes about the show. "I'll think about it," she said to end the conversation. "We'll see."

He smiled. Something about the creases on his forehead and the indentations in his face when his mouth curved made her unable to resist smiling back. Had he been that tall yesterday? Had he bent down when he kissed her, or had she risen up on her toes? He reached into his pocket for a pen and went to her dresser where a hotel notepad lay. "Here's my private number," he said. "Feel honored. I don't give this to anybody."

He straightened and set the pen back in his pocket as his eyes raked over her without hiding their obvious glimmer of attraction. "By the way," he said quietly, "you look great. Forget the television show. This guy'll probably sign you up for the movies."

An unsettling warmth crept up her cheeks. "Thank you," she whispered.

He kept looking down at her, at the soft, billowy hair, at the sharp, polished cotton dress he had ironed, at the blue shoes that matched her fresh eyes. She wet her lips and his heart lurched.

He wanted to kiss her, wanted to taste the raspberry-tinted lip gloss and smell the fragrance of that maddening hair. He wanted to feel her arms slide up around his neck and her breasts crush against his chest.

She saw the desire in his eyes, and her heartbeat accelerated. What was she doing, letting a man like Joe Dillon charm her like some kid just barely on this side of puberty?

What was he doing? he railed inwardly. He wanted a wife, a family. How could he be so serious about those goals one minute, then want desperately to hit on someone as far from wife material as Brit Alexander? He was losing his mind. It must be the stress of all those applications, he thought.

A knock sounded at the door, and Brit gasped. "Oh Lord, I didn't want him to see you here."

Joe shrugged. "I could hide in the bathroom."

Heat mottled her cheeks. "No, that's silly. I'll just tell him you stopped by to...to..."

"To apologize for yesterday," he provided.

"Yes," she said, as if that was as good a lie as any. "To apologize for..."

"Kissing you," he interjected.

She looked up at him, stricken. "No, not that." Her face grew a degree redder. "For...for being so obstinate at the lecture. Yes, that'll work."

"Right," he said. "Obstinate."

Horrified, she caught her breath. "What if he thinks we spent the night together? It's so early..."

"We'll make it clear we didn't," he said. "Don't worry."

The knock sounded again, and she rushed forward. Joe caught her arm and swung her back to him. "Good luck," he whispered, then dropped a kiss on her temple.

Brit's face turned a darker shade of red. She nodded self-consciously, then lurched for the door. "Mr. Halbrook," she said assertively, when she confronted the man who looked exactly as she had pictured him, complete with balding head, protruding paunch and the pungent scent of tobacco.

"Yes," the man said gruffly, taking her extended hand. "I hope I'm not late."

You're five minutes early! she wanted to shout, but instead she said, "No, sir. You're right on time."

Halbrook peered over her shoulder to the recognizable face of the famous Joe Dillon.

Scathing heat burned in Brit's cheeks. "Uh...Mr. Halbrook, this is Joseph Dillon. He was just..."

"Leaving..." Joe said.

"He stopped by a few minutes ago...."

"I was obstinate...." Joe explained too quickly.

"Yes, he was...." Brit added. "Yesterday. He apologized..."

"For being obstinate..." Joe threw in again.

Brit fixed him with a stern look that told him to quit while she was ahead.

"*The* Mr. Dillon?" Halbrook asked dubiously. "The one hunting for a wife?"

"One and the same," Joe said proudly. Brit felt herself shrinking as Halbrook assessed her skeptically.

"Well, I certainly hope our Miss Alexander isn't one of your candidates," he said.

"No, of course not," Joe assured him.

"He's looking for a brunette," Brit added as if the explanation were perfectly logical. "And my parents are divorced."

Confusion pinched the man's grim features, and he nodded slightly. "I see."

"So..." she said, hating the stupid smile on her face as she addressed Joe, but unable to cast it off. "Thanks for coming by, Mr. Dillon. Apology accepted."

He nodded and slipped out the door, smiling awkwardly down at the stern-looking producer. "Well, it was nice meeting you. I have to get home now. Clear the breakfast dishes from my table..."

"Yes," she said. "I'm starving. I would have ordered coffee in the room, but I didn't want a whole pot for just one person."

There, she thought. That ought to assure the man they hadn't spent the night together. Either that, or the overkill would convince him they had and were trying to cover up. "Well, are you ready?" she asked the producer, heart sinking.

"Quite," he said.

Joe nodded again. "Nice to meet you, Mr. Halbrook. And it was good seeing you again, Brit."

Brit felt her face blushing brighter. Halbrook wasn't fooled. He knew... *knew what?* she asked herself. What they had told him was true! Forcing herself not to say another word about it, she closed her door and smiled her most businesslike smile at the producer who could make her dreams come true . . . or squash them like a pack of stale brownies!

Chapter Four

Brit's mother had once told her that first impressions mean very little. She hoped Mr. Halbrook's mother had told him that, too.

It wasn't that the meeting went badly. It just didn't go the way she had planned. He wasn't knocked off his feet, and she still hadn't managed to convince him unequivocally that her show would be a success. After all, there were two strikes against her. The fiasco that the lecture had turned into yesterday, and the fact that he probably believed Joe Dillon had spent the night in her room.

Dropping her purse on the table and kicking off her shoes, she collapsed on the bed, paying no regard to the wrinkles forming in the dress Joe had so carefully ironed. She threw her hand over her eyes and moaned.

Why was that man becoming her downfall when she hardly knew him?

The telephone rang, and she moaned again. It was probably her agent, ready to chew her out for blowing it, or her mother, sitting on the edge of her seat for the verdict. She couldn't face either one of them right now.

But the ringing persisted until finally she snatched up the receiver. "Hello?" she blurted.

"How'd it go?"

The voice wasn't her agent's or her mother's. It was too male. And too sexy. And too familiar.

"Joe, you have got to stop calling me!"

"But this is only the first time."

He had a point, she thought, but that didn't change things. "I don't care. You can't come over, you can't call, I don't want to see your letters and I don't want to write a stupid book." She sat up as her temper escalated. "On second thought, maybe the book is all I'll have to fall back on now that my career is on the rocks, thanks to you."

"Me? What did I do?"

"Plenty," she said.

"I take it the meeting didn't go well."

"Goodbye, Joe." She slammed down the phone and rolled back on the bed, staring at the ceiling.

Immediately, it rang again. She jerked it up, fully intending to slam it down again.

"Don't hang up!" he shouted. "You don't know what I'm going through here. I need your help. Please."

"I can't help you! How can I get that through to you? As my mother always says, 'You made your bed, now you sleep in it.'"

"As I recall, I made *your* bed this morning. Can I sleep in *it*?" The taunting amusement in his voice rankled her.

She sat up, rigid, tempering her voice to sound calm. "Listen carefully, Joe. I don't want you calling me again. I don't want you showing up here with the teeth molds or underwear or G-strings of your latest aspiring wives. Is that clear to you? Can you understand what I'm saying?"

"Loud and clear," he said, undaunted. "But what I called to tell you is that I'm sending Jerome to pick you up at seven. I'm cooking dinner for you. See you then."

"Joe, I am not—" The phone went dead in her hand, and she screamed in frustration. She stared at the phone, pretending it was his throat, and throttled it. Then she banged it back into its cradle and lay back down. The man was in serious mental trouble, she thought, because hell would freeze over before she would go to Joe's house for dinner!

The temperature dropped unexpectedly late that afternoon, and Brit surmised that it must be rather cold in the underworld.

But that wasn't why she was considering going to Joe's. She was considering it—only considering it— because her agent insisted that this book idea might not be so farfetched, after all. It might give her bargaining power with Halbrook, she had said, make her more valuable, and it certainly gave her a more believable alibi for having been with him this morning.

What really riled her was that he fully expected her to come! Just as he fully expected to find a wife in a pile of strange letters and stale brownies.

All afternoon she had tried to forget the arrogance of the invitation, even while she gave her lecture to the women of Emory University. Hours later it still irked her, and her agent's stand on the situation didn't help matters any.

She yanked a brush through her hair, threw it down, then went to the closet. Maybe she would go, making sure he understood it was strictly business and that she had no intention of becoming a little diversion while he searched for a wife. She'd set him straight once and for all. And she'd do it in red, her best color.

Hold it! she thought, hauling her thoughts back. She would not do it in red. She would wear a pair of jeans and a black pullover sweater that made her complexion look like death. See if he wanted to keep seeing her after that!

By the time she had dressed, however, she had compromised. Jeans and a red pullover sweater. After all, he *had* been subjected to the robe this morning. She didn't want him to think she was a frumpy old hag.

What did she care what he thought? her inner voice argued. His opinion didn't matter at all. No, she decided unequivocally. She was not going to have dinner with Joe. She would send Jerome away when he came for her.

When seven came, she was sitting cross-legged on her bed, watching a sitcom on television. Jerome could come up and get her, she thought, and she'd absolutely refuse to go. The idea was immensely satisfying.

At five minutes before seven, the telephone rang. "This is Mr. Cory at the front desk," the voice said. "Your driver is waiting for you in the lobby."

"Let me speak to him," she said.

The man put her on hold, then came back to the phone. "I'm sorry, Miss Alexander, but I don't see him at the moment. The lobby is crowded...."

"Never mind," she said. "I'll come down and tell him."

Brit hung up and grabbed her purse and room key, knowing Jerome was probably following Joe's orders. He probably thought making her come down gave him more of an edge in convincing her to come and that if Jerome came up he might never get her out of her room.

With chin held high in determination, she rode down to the lobby and looked around for Jerome. There was no sign of him. Confused, she went to the front desk, scanning the name tags for Mr. Cory. "Excuse me, sir," she said when she found him. "I was supposed to meet my driver, but he doesn't seem to be here."

The man nodded toward the front doors. "I found him right after we hung up," he told her. "He said he'd meet you in the limousine."

Brit bit her lip. So this was how they would play it, huh? Bait and lure... bait and lure... She considered going right back to her room, but couldn't resist seeing Jerome's face when she let him know Joe's bullying methods would not work on her.

Several cabs lined the sidewalk, but only one limousine, and Jerome wasn't the driver behind the wheel. Now what? she asked herself.

Suddenly someone tapped on her shoulder, and she spun around to confront Joe Dillon grinning his most disarming grin at her. "Hi," he said.

"I'm not going with you." It seemed necessary to get that out right away. She glanced around. "I thought you were sending Jerome."

"I forgot it was Thursday. He does Hamlet on Thursday nights and weekends."

"Then I'm *sure* not going," she said, as if there'd ever been any doubt. "With your driving record—"

"I'm not driving. This is my rented limo," he said, "chauffeur and all."

She glanced at the black limo, then back to Joe towering over her with that maddening plea on his face. "It doesn't matter, Joe. I'm still not going."

"But I'm barbecuing," he said, as if that settled things. "Besides, I'm getting close to the end of my search. I've narrowed it down a lot."

Something in her chest tightened. "To how many?" she asked grudgingly.

He shrugged. "Maybe fifty or so. I thought you might have a more objective eye. You could help weed them out."

"No," she said. "Let Jerome help you."

"I can't," he told her. "I can't trust his motives. He wants the good ones for himself. But for less honorable reasons."

"I'll bet," she said. "Only I imagine when you get right down to it, your reasons aren't all that much more honorable than his."

He went to the car door and opened it. She didn't budge.

"What is it you're afraid of?" he asked.

"It won't work," she said. "You used the challenge tactic yesterday, remember?"

"It worked then." A slow grin sauntered across his face. "But really, are you nervous around me? Am I that hard to get along with?"

"No, I'm not nervous," she lied.

"Then come help me. What's the big deal? It's not like I'm going to propose to you or anything. I'm sort of taken. As I see it, we're both pretty safe from each other."

The thought was too unsettling, even if it were true on some intellectual level. She sighed and looked back toward the hotel doors.

"What's your alternative?" he asked. "Sitting in the room watching sitcoms?"

"Relaxing," she said. "I've had a hard day."

"Relax at my house," he urged. "I promise, you'll enjoy it. If not, I'll bring you right back."

At his signal, the driver cranked the engine. Joe stood at the door, gesturing for her to get in. People were beginning to stare. A few people who seemed to recognize the renowned man had stopped at their cabs' doors, meters running, to watch the scene. Finally, to avoid drawing any more attention, Brit mouthed a mild curse and got into the car.

Joe Dillon loaded the last dish into the dishwasher, dried his hands and went to the doorway of his study. She had grown very quiet in there since dinner, he thought. The first few applications, once again, had infuriated her, but now she seemed to be studying them intently, taking notes on a legal pad he'd given her.

She sat in the leather chair behind his desk, her legs thrown over the arm, with a pile of letters in her lap. Occasionally she checked the computer to see what the program had said about the subject she was studying. Her soft golden hair cascaded down into her face, half hiding it from his scrutiny. Those eyes were luminous in the lamplight, doing something odd to his heart. His eyes moved lower, to the red knit sweater bulking over her jeans. Did she know how good she looked in red? he wondered. His eyes traveled over those long legs to the fuzzy striped socks she wore on her feet. Her shoes had long ago dropped to the floor.

He leaned back against the doorjamb and watched her. She was alone and quiet and completely at peace with herself. Why couldn't he enjoy being alone the way she obviously did? Why couldn't he be fulfilled as a bachelor?

Because he wanted more, he thought. He wanted to know that someone was somewhere in his house, padding around in fuzzy socks and a terry-cloth robe, with rollers in her hair. He wanted to get used to that special scent of her skin and the warmth of her body next to his at night. There was no reason he should have to do without when other men had it.

His deep sigh drew her head up, and their eyes met across the lamplit expanse of room. For a moment their gazes locked, quietly, soberly, almost sadly. A faint smile softened his lips.

"How's it going?"

She looked back down at the applications. "You won't like it," she said. "I'm afraid I've shot holes in most of these."

Joe lifted a chair by its top rung and set it down beside her. "Let's see."

She handed him the first. "Mandy Salinger," she said.

Joe nodded. "Yeah. She was in the top ten on the computer."

"Shows you how much the computer knows," Brit observed.

"What do you mean?"

"Well, look at this." She handed him a list of discrepancies she had found. "None of her information jibes. She said she grew up in the Air Force in Holland, but I happen to know that this town she cites isn't anywhere near an Air Force base. And right here she says she's the only girl of seven children. Six brothers, yet she doesn't play any sports. Does that seem odd to you? Also, if she has six brothers, why does she have to answer an ad for a husband? Every girl I know with brothers has plenty of possibilities."

Joe looked a little insulted. "A person doesn't have to be hard up to look for a spouse in an ad, you know." He studied the application again. "Says she has a master's degree in home economics."

"Then why is she working in a factory? She could be teaching home ec."

"Maybe she makes more money doing that."

"Or maybe she lied and told you what you wanted to hear."

Joe sighed and tossed that letter aside. "Okay, you win. One down. What about this one?"

Brit scanned the one he offered her, refreshing her memory. "Oh, yes. Hilga. Well, this should be obvious, even to you."

"What?" he asked. "She seems fine. She's pretty, well educated, well traveled...."

"She speaks Russian!" Brit sputtered.

"So what?"

"So she's obviously probably a spy."

Joe's loud laughter irritated her further. "Obviously probably? Is that the best you can do?"

Brit lifted her chin, indignant. "Fine," she said. "Marry her, then try explaining to your children why their mother is in prison for treason."

He covered his mouth as his chortle rolled out, and dropped the file with the other discard. "Okay, Brit.

You win. I couldn't possibly consider someone who's so obviously probably a spy." His laughter faded, and he wiped his eyes. "All right. What's wrong with this one? Says she's a novelist. Must be a deep thinker."

"You can't be serious about marrying some woman who just sits around daydreaming all day and writes about life instead of living it!"

"Right," Joe chuckled, dropping that one with the others. "What could I have been thinking? Let's see, that still leaves forty-seven choices."

One by one she knocked out each choice, stating reasons that seemed obvious to her and vague, if not hysterical, to him. Hours passed as they worked, but Joe kept her glass filled with wine.

It was near midnight when they got down to the last few, the ones Brit hadn't been able to find fault with. She lay sideways on the couch, her feet propped in Joe's lap, a warm buzz in her head.

"Sheila Hamer," Joe said with a yawn. "Give it your best shot. What's wrong with her?"

"Her comments are too pat," Brit said. "It's almost like she thought for hours over each one. It's suspicious."

"Well, I certainly hope she thought over each one. I wanted honest answers."

"These comments couldn't be honest. That's what I'm saying."

"How could you know that?"

"They're too perfect, that's why."

"Out of eight thousand applicants, you don't think I could find one who has what I'm looking for? And if I remember, this one made great brownies."

"Fine," she said, dropping her feet from his lap and sitting up. "If you want to marry a brownie machine, go ahead."

Joe slapped the application on the cushion next to him. "I just don't see what you want."

"It isn't what *I* want that matters here, Joe. It's what *you* want. And if you want someone like that…"

"Someone who fits every one of my requirements, is attractive, has decent values and *wants* to get married as badly as I do?"

"Suit yourself," she said with a shrug as she surveyed the amount of wine left in her glass. "What do I care if you wake up one morning and find that this woman who looks so good on paper is really a lazy whelp who neglects her children and henpecks you into misery?"

"*How* in the world did you get all that from this flawless letter?"

"That's the point," she said, coming to her feet and slinging her hair back over her shoulder. "Flawless. That was exactly the word I was looking for!"

"Flawless is *bad*?" he asked.

She threw a long-suffering look to the ceiling, then focused on him again. "People aren't real unless they have flaws, Joe. You live with Miss Sunshine long enough and you'll wish you'd found someone who had a few things wrong with her."

Vexation growing, Joe sifted through the piles on the floor. "Well, let's see. I could have any number of flawed women here, according to you. Here's a pathological liar. Oh, look! Why don't I marry this over-educated prude? I know. I'll marry this one with the knife scar on her cheek. Is that flawed enough for you?"

He abandoned the stack, stood up, and jerked the ten she hadn't been able to roast out of her hands. "Come on, Brit. Look through these again. Surely you can find at least one flaw here. If you can't, make them up like you did with the others!"

"I did not make them up. You asked for my help and I gave it to you."

"You want flaws?" he asked, closing in on her. She stepped backward, felt the wall at her back. "How about a fire-spitting blonde who doesn't need a husband, but is dead set on making sure I don't find a wife?"

"That's not fair," she whispered. "I didn't ask to come here."

He moved closer, but she couldn't back away. His voice dropped in pitch and volume, but that underlying note of anger still pulsed through it. "How about a woman who walks around in a frayed terry-cloth robe in the mornings with half of her hair in rollers? How about a woman who loses her shoes and leaves her dresser cluttered with makeup?"

She swallowed and looked up at him, her heart responding to what was becoming more sensuous whisper than angry accusation. She felt his breath on her lips, felt the warm length of his body barely brushing hers, felt his eyes probing much too deeply into her soul.

"Are those the kinds of flaws you're talking about?" he whispered.

She opened her mouth to answer, but the parting of her lips seemed to have another purpose. Slowly, she felt him moving closer. His eyes meshed with hers, as his lips narrowed the distance between them. "Don't," she whispered, but he paid her no heed.

When his lips touched hers, her heart lurched, then fluttered back into place. His gentleness frightened her, threatened her. She felt the midnight stubble of his jaw, smelled the faint scent of soap mingled with the room's own smell of fresh bare wood. He was strength where she was weakness, faith where she was doubt, fantasy where she was reality.

Her hands slid up his chest, over the heart hammering urgently against her fingertips. She had forged a life for herself alone, and she didn't want company. But a hunger grew up inside her that she hadn't experienced before. A warm, hot hunger that surpassed her previous fulfillment, a hunger that said there was more....

Overwhelmed, she broke the kiss and gazed up into his smoky black eyes, silently pleading with him to make her feel separate again, detached. But he had felt the hunger, too.

"I don't think I want any of those women," he whispered, his voice husky against her face. "I think you're right about them. They're not what I want."

She couldn't answer. All she could manage was to swallow the lump in her throat.

His eyes swept down to her lips, and a gentle hand cupped her chin. "What if I gave it up?" he asked. "What if we—you and I—started seeing each other?"

"No," she whispered, breathless. Her heartbeat accelerated. "If you were an ordinary man, maybe. But you aren't. You want a wife. I don't want a husband. I like my life the way it is. I like waking up alone in the mornings and not having to cook at night if I don't want to. I like traveling and being free to pick up and go. I don't have room in my life for anyone tying me down." She saw the sparkle in his eyes, the yearning, and knew he wasn't convinced. "Besides, I'm nothing like what you want."

As if he hadn't heard, his mouth claimed hers again, erasing the arguments from her mind, leaving her disarmed and defenseless. He coaxed her mouth open as he pressed against her. He tasted of wine and Joe, a unique taste she would never forget, and his arms around her made her feel small. But she didn't want to feel small.

She pushed away again, but he kept his forehead pressed against hers. "Maybe what I thought I wanted isn't really what I want," he whispered. "Maybe I'm tired of brownie-baking brunettes."

"You can't abandon this for me," she said.

"If I'd met you first," he said, "maybe I never would have started it."

She shook her head, growing more nervous the more certain he sounded. "I'm not wife material, Joe.

I'll never fit any of your requirements. I told you," she whispered, still breathless, "I even flunked Spanish."

"I only listed that because I thought it would show intelligence," he said. "I already know you're smart." He kissed her forehead, breathed a deep sigh and chuckled against her face. "Besides, you can always learn. Anyway," he whispered, still chuckling maddeningly against her ear, "sometimes a man has to compromise. Sometimes he just has to lower his standards a little."

Brit's backbone went rigid and she glared up at him, disbelief etched in the lines that now painted fury rather than laughter on her expression. "What did you say?"

"I said—"

"Never mind. I heard you." She slipped out of his arms, went into the desk for the ten final letters and slapped them into his hand. "No need to lower your standards for me, Joe, when you can have the best. Go ahead, find a wife. I hope you'll be happy."

"Aw, Brit, I was just kidding. That's not what I meant."

"I know exactly what you meant." She snatched up her purse. "And don't expect me to come back here. If I decide to write the book, you can box up the letters and send them to me after you're finished. I don't think I want to help you with this anymore."

"That's okay," he said. "I don't think you can be all that objective, anyway."

"And what is that supposed to mean!"

"Just that maybe you don't *really* want me to find a wife. Maybe deep down you know that as long as you keep finding fault, I'll keep coming to you."

She pointed a shaking finger at him. "You, Joseph Dillon, are a jackass! And I'm about to put an end to any theory you have about what I feel *deep down*!"

"And you said *I* was obstinate!"

Brit didn't honor the comment with an answer. She merely stormed out of the house and to the limo, where the driver slept at the wheel. She knocked loudly on the window, startling him into wakefulness. "Please take me back to my hotel," she clipped.

"Won't Mr. Dillon be coming?" he asked, rubbing his eyes.

"Not if he values his life," she murmured, slamming into the back seat and locking all the doors. "The jerk!"

Mutely, the driver started the car and pulled out of the gravel drive.

Chapter Five

Joe lay in bed that night, staring at the rough-hewn, twenty-foot ceiling. It was all he could do to keep from calling her, but he had his principles to consider. The lady wasn't interested, and that was all there was to it.

He turned over and beat his pillow, then buried his face in it. Her response when he kissed her came back to him, despite how he fought it. He had felt the tension easing out of her muscles, her accelerated heartbeat, her strained breathing. She had tasted like warmth and happiness and woke every sense stirring in his body. And she didn't give a whit about his money or his name.

She was no Diana.

He rolled back over and threw his wrist over his eyes. Damn it, why had he even bothered to compare? Hadn't he known that when measured against the woman who had almost made him swear off women once and for all, Brit would come out miles ahead of her? She made his need for a wife seem less an obsession and more a yearning in his soul. God, he had lousy timing. If he hadn't been on this wife-hunt, he might have met her some other way, made her fall in love with him without even knowing it. But it could never happen this way. She was too guarded. Too wary.

He closed his eyes and thought he smelled her scent on his hands. He had run those hands through her soft locks of hair, had touched her pulsating neck, had held her, warm and supple, against him. And now he was supposed to write her off, as if he'd never met her?

He sat up in bed and flicked on the lamp, sending a yellow glow climbing the papered walls. Bending his legs, he set his elbows on his knees and raked his fingers through his hair. What was he thinking? He wanted a wife, a family, and he intended to have one. But not just anyone. The *right* one. And the day hadn't yet come when he'd stop fighting for what he wanted. That day would never come.

A slow smile dawned across his face as the first pink rays of sunlight drifted through the window. Yes, he still knew how to fight. And somehow he'd get what he wanted.

The fury Brit had felt upon leaving Joe's house that night diminished in intensity and grew more distant as days passed without a word. He hadn't called as she'd expected, hadn't shown up at her hotel, hadn't even sent his Brooklyn Hamlet to iron things out. It was almost as if he had seen the light and realized she wasn't worth his time. Strangely, it left her suspended in a peculiar limbo she couldn't explain.

But Wednesday morning, as she was on her way out the door to register the students for her first Atlanta seminar at Georgia State, the phone rang. Her stomach flip-flopped as it had each time the phone had rung since that night. Each time her spirits sagged inexplicably when it was only her mother or her agent or a friend from home.

This time, however, it was Joe.

"I can't talk right now," she said, feeling a strange quivering in her chest. "I'm on my way to the campus to register my class."

"It won't take long," he said in a cool voice. "I just wanted to let you know there's no need to worry about that silly little idea I had the other night about calling off my search so that you and I could see each other."

"I wasn't worried," she said, her heart sinking. "I knew you couldn't have meant it."

"Yeah, well. Guess I just lost my head. The heat of the moment, you know? I'm back on track now." He sighed meaningfully, and something within her plunged. "It's full-speed ahead. I've stepped up my advertising, and I'm hiring some help to get this all on computer. I feel myself getting closer."

"Thank you for sharing that with me," she said through compressed lips. "I'll sleep better now."

"Good." He paused a moment, and her mind conjured a grudging picture of him. He was probably in his study, she thought, and the scent of wood probably dominated the air. His dark hair was probably tousled and hanging in his eyes. He was probably wearing a flannel shirt and a pair of faded jeans, and he probably had his bare feet propped up....

"So, how's it going with your seminar?" he asked.

"We're only registering tonight. I won't be starting the seminars until next Saturday. I have lectures all next week."

"Oh. Well, how's it going with your television show? Did you convince the producer yet?"

She breathed an irritated breath and wondered if he really cared. "I'm having dinner with him Saturday night, not that it's any of your business."

"Dinner, huh? Well, good luck."

"Thank you."

Silence stretched over the line, and Brit asked herself why she didn't just hang up. There was really nothing more to say. She could just say goodbye, return the receiver to its cradle and forget she'd ever met him...or kissed him....

"Well," he said finally, his voice slightly hoarse, "guess I'd better get back to the applications before I go in to work. I've decided to call some of them today. See if we can meet."

Brit lowered to her bed and felt her face turning pale.

"Yeah, I'm gonna be spending some time with them. It's a dirty business, this wife-hunting, but somebody's got to do it."

Brit found no amusement in what he'd said, and there was none in his voice. "Good luck," she whispered. "I hope you find what you're looking for."

"I always do," he said. "It's just a matter of knowing how to go after it."

Another stretch of silence followed, and finally Brit heard the steady hum of the dial tone invading their time. Quietly, she hung up. So he was getting closer to finding the woman he wanted. She was very happy for him. Really. She was.

What's wrong with you? she asked herself. It wasn't as if *she* wanted him. There wasn't room in her life for him. It was best that she was rid of him once and for all.

She left the hotel and got her rented car. She'd pulled to the edge of the parking lot waiting for the traffic to let up when her eyes strayed to a billboard across the street, where two men were busy plastering up the newest product to be advertised. Two kind black eyes glistened from the billboard, startling her, and she watched, frozen, as the men rolled on the rest of the face... Joe's face.

The caption hanging from the scaffolding, not yet pasted up, said, "Lonely? Brunette? Educated? Uncle Joe Wants *You*."

Slamming her foot on the accelerator, Brit screeched out of the parking lot and seethed all the way to the campus.

* * *

"Life's nothing but a picnic that got rained on after the ants took over anyway," Lana Bell Lawrence drawled in a syrupy southern accent. She was half lying on the registration table next to Brit. "I thought divorce was going to free me. Instead, I just traded one set of chains for another."

Brit laughed at the university secretary who had been assigned to work at her table. Idly, she counted the stack of her last rush of registrants. Seventy-five, and they were just up to the Js—that meant there would be a second seminar at this college alone. Already, she calculated, with her college lectures and weekend seminars, she'd be in town at least six weeks, and that was only if the TV show fell through. She wondered if the town was big enough for her and Joe Dillon for that long. She glanced over at the forlorn secretary whose life seemed to be on a downswing. "Aren't you being a little melodramatic about this?"

"Melodramatic? Hmph. That's easy for you to say. You have confidence. You have clout. You have charisma." Lana Bell leaned over the table and examined a polished fingernail. "Shoot, you probably even have credit."

"Yes, my dear," Brit said in a proper mock-British voice. "And all those things can be yours in two easy lessons."

Lana Bell sighed. "I'm a working girl, Brit. I can't just take off for two days...."

Brit wasn't fooled. "You're off on Saturday and Sunday, anyway."

"I'm hopeless," Lana went on. "You probably couldn't do anything for me."

"Oh, ye of little faith. I once took an airheaded stripper from Bourbon Street and turned her into the chairman of the board of a Fortune 500 company."

Lana threw Brit a skeptical look. "Is that what is commonly referred to as a minor exaggeration?"

Brit's lips twitched. "More like a major one," she confessed. "But come to my seminar and I personally guarantee you clout, confidence, charisma and credit by the time you leave. All at the everyday low price of a hundred and fifty dollars."

"If I had a hundred and fifty dollars I'd buy that pair of Italian shoes I saw at Macy's and get my hair done!" Lana Bell leaned back, stretching her arms over her fuzzy red head. "And if there was any left over, I'd buy a new silver dress and amble on down to the nearest singles' bar to find me a nice-looking guy who could sweep me off my feet and love me till I lose my mind."

Brit shook her head dolefully. "Lana Bell, woman cannot live on love alone."

"Ever tried it?" Lana Bell asked with a devilish grin.

Brit gave her a disgusted look. "All right, Lana Bell. You can sit in on my seminar for free. I consider you someone who is in desperate need of my services."

Lana Bell laughed and stretched like a lazy feline. "I'll be there," she said. "Oh, and can I bring a date?"

Brit leered at her, then turned her attention to the new rush of registrants coming into the gym.

"Oh, my God," Lana Bell drawled. "It's the Ks through Ms. Look out, they're a rowdy bunch."

Brit couldn't help giggling at the crowd of women who'd been waiting to be let in, and she thanked her stars that Lana Bell had helped to get her mind off wife-hunts, ads in newspapers, compromises and seductive billboards.

By the end of the day Brit had registered 155 students, enough for four seminars since she only allowed 40 per class. Her stay in Atlanta was getting longer and longer, she realized with some discomfort. It would mean being in constant contact with that stupid billboard if not with Joe Dillon himself. But it also meant she'd seem more successful in Mr. Halbrook's eyes.

They were packing up the cards and boxes when a delivery boy rushed into the gym. "A package for Ms. Alexander," he called.

"I'm Ms. Alexander," she said. The young man came closer and handed her a small box and a clipboard to sign. "Who's it from?" she asked.

The young man grinned. "Just says 'A Secret Admirer.'"

Lana Bell's head snapped up. "A secret admirer, huh? Let me see that."

She jerked the wrapped gift out of Brit's hand and shook it. "It's too flat to be a ring, doesn't smell like perfume, isn't ticking...."

Brit handed the clipboard back to the messenger and took the gift. "It's got to be a joke," she said. "I don't have any secret admirer...." Her voice trailed off as she read the wrapping and saw a cassette tape that read, "Conversational French Made Simple." Blood suffused her cheeks and she dropped into her chair.

"Conversational French?" Lana Bell blurted, crestfallen. "What kind of romantic gift is that?" She took the cassette, turned it over. "Hey, look, there's a note attached. Says, 'It's never too late to learn.' What is that supposed to mean?"

Brit sighed heavily. "It means that I have this lingering headache that won't quit," she said. "And it's likely to last until I get out of this town."

Brit wished for a different entrance into her hotel's parking lot that evening to avoid looking in the eye of the man looming on the billboard, but none magically appeared. He was trying to drive her crazy, she thought, trying to torture her slowly. She would tell him to leave her alone if she spoke to him again. She would send back his French tape and let him know that she had no intention of learning to speak a foreign language for any man.

Still, she couldn't seem to resist putting the cassette in her rented car's tape deck and halfheartedly repeating, *"Je parle français. Je ne suis pas française. Je viens de Boston."* She caught herself in midsentence as the foreign voice began chanting "How are you" and "I am fine." He had done it to her again! Forced her to feel a way she didn't want to feel! It was

like when he'd kissed her and almost made her want
to belong to him and explore the feeling further. He
had no right to manipulate her that way!

She jerked the tape out, threw it across the car and,
careful to keep her eyes averted from the gigantic billboard, pulled into a parking space. She would not
think of him again! Not even if he were the last man
on earth.

Joe Dillon wasn't the last man on earth, but from
the way the newspapers touted him, one would have
thought he was at least the last available bachelor. His
first "interview date" hit the papers with more hoopla
than the tornado that had destroyed a twenty-mile
stretch of homes. The society page of the *Atlanta
Constitution* gave a brief background on the marriage candidate Joe had chosen to meet in person. Brit
recognized her as one of the sleazily dressed ones that
hung on his wall, though she did look quite a bit more
presentable in the newspaper photograph.

He had his arm around her and was laughing with
genuine delight, though he looked right into the camera, almost as if mocking Brit directly or daring her to
object.

That night Brit lay in bed, exhausted but unable to
sleep as thoughts of Joe with that...that *impostor*...racked her mind. He probably believed, in his
naive way, that this woman who fit the bill of Holly-
wood starlet better than wife or mother was really
what he was looking for. The floozy probably really
had him fooled.

Poor Joe, she thought, as sleep finally began to pull her under its current. Poor, naive Joe...

Joe Dillon sat across the table from the second of his "interview dates," Sue Ann, again taken directly from the wall, instead of from the "ten most likely" he and Brit had narrowed down, or the dozens of others his computer had chosen. He propped his chin on his hand and tried to look interested in the woman's conversation. Although it was nearly midnight, he knew it was more than the lateness of the hour that was making his eyelids droop.

"And Mavis—that's my next-door neighbor— Mavis says, she says, 'I can't see how you can really want to marry some man you've never even seen,' and I just looked at her like this and said, 'Well, somebody in this life has to take chances now and then. I mean, good things don't just fall into your lap. You got to work for them.' Just like my mama said about the Miss Georgia pageant, she said, 'Honey, the ones who win are the ones who enter.' Well, I never won Miss Georgia or nothin', but I figured it was the same with this. I mean, you sure as heck won't get picked if you don't go for it. I mean, *c'est la vie*, you know? That's French. Did I tell you I speak French and Australian?"

Joe nodded and tried to filter his yawn through his nostrils. He wondered if Brit had been incensed by the cassette tape he'd sent her today, just to let her know the door wasn't completely closed if she chose to open it. He chuckled lightly, right on cue for something Sue

Ann had just said—something she had meant to be
funny. He didn't give a darn whether or not Brit could
speak French. The tape had just been his way of getting a rise out of her.

He glanced around the restaurant, wondering if the
photographers had all left. God, he hoped so, so that
he could take this woman home and tell her, in the
nicest way he could, "Don't call me, I'll call you." At
least the picture in the paper would keep Brit's blood
rushing. He'd half expected a furious phone call this
evening, when she saw the paper with the pictures
from last night's date. Good grief, he thought dolefully. Only the second date, and already he was tiring
of it.

But he'd better try to have more fun, he thought.
Because Brit wasn't likely to change her mind, and he
hadn't given up on his wife-hunt. One way or another, he was going to get what he wanted. But Sue
Ann didn't happen to be it. Damn, how he wished
she'd talk about something interesting, like nuclear
war or the state of the stock market or the price of a
head of lettuce. Anything but this incessant rambling
about his wife-hunt.

"And when you called me yesterday, well, I about
died, but I thought, why not? It's sort of in my destiny. I believe in destiny, you know, because I'm a
Sagittarius, and Sagittarians are..."

Joe wondered where Brit was tonight. She hadn't
mentioned plans. Maybe she was practicing up on her
French, he thought with a wry grin. Or maybe she was
out. Maybe he should have drilled her a little more. All

he knew of her plans this weekend was that she was going out with her producer on Saturday night. Maybe it would be worth a phone call or two to find out where they'd be. Maybe...

"And my mama was just tickled about your electronics company. I mean, all those little gadgets and things. You must just be so smart to be able to think of all those things to sell...."

Joe signaled for the waiter and decided to call it a night.

The restaurant that Mr. Halbrook had chosen for his dinner with Brit and her agent, Eugenia, who had flown into Atlanta that afternoon, was, ironically, an exquisitely converted church called The Abbey, in which the waiters were dressed in monks' robes and spoke in French accents to complement the expensive French cuisine. Halbrook seemed to be in better spirits than he had after her breakfast with him days ago. For one reason, Joe Dillon was nowhere in sight, and Brit could concentrate on selling herself and her program instead of covering for some night-long rendezvous that hadn't even taken place.

Brit had tried to avoid the newspapers for the past two days, though she felt herself gravitating toward them each time she saw one. The glimpses she caught of Joe with his latest interest tantalized her, until she had no choice but to read about his date and seethe and fume and huff.

But tonight he was the furthest thing from her mind, she told herself. Her career was on an upswing. And she might as well get used to Joe Dillon, because she would be spending a lot of time in Atlanta when she started doing her show. She'd grow immune to the billboards and the newspaper articles, and when he finally chose his wife...

"I'm impressed with the registration in your seminars here," Mr. Halbrook was saying. "Do you have this much response in every city?"

"Sometimes more," she said. "Last year I stayed in New York for three months."

"Toronto ran ten weeks," Eugenia added. "People flock to her. She gives women a sense of being able to do anything. The letters we get are astounding. If they're any indication of the questions she'll get on her show, the ratings will be sky-high."

Halbrook tapped a cigarette in his hand, then groped in his pocket for a match. "I'm mostly concerned about image," he said. "As you know, advertisers are very fickle people. Any hint of a drop in credibility and they run like a rabbit from a greyhound. I'll be frank with you." He paused to light his cigarette, then narrowed his eyes and studied his stout drink. After a moment he peered at her from under eyebrows so thick Brit could have cleaned her venetian blinds with them. "I'm concerned about your relationship with Mr. Dillon."

"Mr. Dillon?" she asked, feeling suddenly as if he had seen right through her and read her thoughts. "*Joe* Dillon?"

"Yes," Halbrook said. "I'm concerned that people will... misinterpret your relationship."

Brit gave Eugenia a beseeching look, then looked back at the producer. "There is no relationship, Mr. Halbrook. I'm simply considering writing a book about his search for a wife when he's done."

Eugenia piped in in her calmest professional tone. "I understand his letters from women are fascinating. We think that it would be an interesting study for Brit to conduct. These women represent the small facet of American women who still believe that only a man can fulfill them."

Brit leaned forward to make her points more clearly. "Mr. Halbrook, I never try to convince a woman there's anything *wrong* with having a man in her life. I simply try to make her understand that she should be her own person, find her own fulfillment, *before* she becomes part of a couple. I stress that a woman shouldn't depend on anyone else for her self-worth. It starts inside her. If she finds it there, she can be successful in any arena, even marriage. But she won't see marriage as the be-all and end-all, and she won't feel that she's a failure if it isn't for her." She sipped her drink and allowed her speech to soak in. "Mr. Dillon's applicants represent the women I most need to reach. That's why I'm considering—only considering—writing the book. But even if I decide to do it, my contact with Mr. Dillon will probably be non-existent."

"Yes," Eugenia threw in. "The man will probably be married by the time Brit starts work on it. He'll give her the letters and be done with them."

Brit felt herself bristling at the reminder. Why were they talking about this, anyway? Joe had agreed to the book only if she helped him narrow his choices, and she had no intention of doing that again. The book would never even happen.

Her eyes wandered as Eugenia and Mr. Halbrook went on about the concept of Brit's show. Her focus slid around the room where tailored businessmen sat in quiet conversation with other men or women; it swept the tables where French dishes lay, their smells wafting on the air; it passed the door, where a tall dark-haired man with a brunette was slipping the maître d' a hundred-dollar bill—

Brit's eyes screeched back to the door, and she felt her jaw dropping to her chest. Joe Dillon grinned his most innocent smile and waved across the room. Brit sat, frozen, as the maître d' led him to the empty table next to her!

Chapter Six

Well, well, well," Joe Dillon said in mock surprise as Brit gaped up at him. "Is it a small world or what?"

Without taking her eyes from him, Brit muttered, "Mr. Halbrook, I think you've met Joe Dillon."

"Yes, Mr. Halbrook," Joe said, his forehead wrinkled in too-apparent delight as he extended his hand. "Oh, and this is my date, Kitty Hopkins."

"Hello," the woman said in a husky bedroom voice.

Slowly, Brit glanced past Joe to the hussy whose letter she had watched him open the other night—the one whose panties had seemed just another annoyance to him until he'd seen her picture. "Hi…Kitty." Despite her determination to appear indifferent, Brit gave the woman a head-to-toe assessment and felt her cheeks searing in pink patches. Kitty's name fit her well, for the way she stood, in her porn queen's stance with her tight black leather dress unzipped to well beneath her ample cleavage, reminded Brit of the female version of a tomcat on the prowl. What could she possibly say to the woman? *You have lovely taste in undergarments? Don't your lips get tired of staying puckered that way? Don't look now, but your dress has come unzipped?*

Before Brit could choose the best of the bungling lines that rushed to mind, a team of photographers stampeded in and began flashing pictures. Joe waved obligingly at the cameras, as if the band of reporters was the party he'd come here to meet. Perfectly on cue, Kitty purred and rubbed against him.

The waiters in their monks' robes bustled toward the photographers in horror, while the maître d' sputtered furiously, "I'm *really* going to have to ask you people to leave! You really mustn't do this here!"

Joe seemed oblivious to the uproar he was causing and continued smiling for the cameras until the last of the photographers was escorted out. Then, as if the entire restaurant full of diners weren't staring at him flabbergasted, he picked up the conversation where it had left off.

"I'm sorry," he said to Eugenia. "I don't believe we've met."

Go away! Brit wanted to scream. *Go get your cat a saucer of milk and a nice rug to sharpen her claws on!* But remembering she was trying to make a good impression on Mr. Halbrook, she forced herself to remain genial while straining the very boundaries of politeness.

"This is Eugenia, my agent," Brit said. "We were discussing business."

Her coldness seemed only to entertain him. "Oh, don't let me interrupt," he said. "Kitty and I have some business of our own to discuss, don't we, Kitty?"

Again, Kitty purred and rubbed against him.

"Would you believe the maître d' seated us right next to your table?"

"Will wonders never cease?" Brit asked sarcastically, looking daggers at the greedy maître d'.

Joe bent to her ear, his voice a whispered rumble. "Don't worry about us bothering you. We'll be talking quietly. By the way, you ought to taste this girl's brownies."

"I thought you threw them away," she grated.

He snickered quietly. "She let me sample a fresh batch."

For a moment, Brit wondered if the whites of her eyes were turning red or if smoke were wafting out of her ears. She watched, angry at herself as she did, while Joe seated the feline floozy at the table behind Brit and cuddled up next to her.

"You're right," Eugenia muttered absently as she gaped at them. "He *is* gorgeous."

The declaration was like a left hook that startled Brit back to her senses. What could Mr. Halbrook be thinking? "I never said that," Brit corrected, mentally murdering her agent.

"You were thinking it, though," Eugenia said.

Brit decided her best bet was to forget Eugenia and go to work on the producer. Plastering on her brightest smile, she tried to look relaxed. "Well, as you can see, Mr. Halbrook, Joe Dillon's search for a wife is progressing nicely. You have nothing to fear where I'm concerned."

"Yes, I can see that." Halbrook couldn't seem to keep his eyes from the couple whispering and giggling into each other's ears. "I'd say he's just about made his choice."

Brit couldn't resist glancing back over her shoulder. Joe had his arm around the lady—if one could indeed call her that—and was close enough to assess the scent of her lipstick or her toothpaste or study the condition of her teeth. Brit jerked her head back to Mr. Halbrook. "I don't think he'd *marry* her. She's not Joe's type at all. She's too...too..."

"Too well endowed?" Eugenia asked on a chuckle.

"No," she said. "Joe's looking for a wife. Not a sex kitten. He wants someone who will be a good mother to his children. Not some husky-voiced hoyden—"

"A lot can be said for husky-voiced hoydens," Halbrook said, his eyes growing wider at the view he was getting of the woman's legs.

Chagrined, Brit sat more stiffly in her chair. "Could we get back to the television show, please? Perhaps we need to remind ourselves that we've been talking about a show that would make comments like that a little less acceptable, especially for its producer."

Mr. Halbrook cleared his throat and rubbed at his smile. "Sorry. I suppose it was uncalled-for."

Brit nodded acceptance and let out a heavy breath while she attempted to focus her thoughts. "I was thinking that for the first two or three shows we should solicit the phone calls from former seminar students of mine, or people who have written to me. After that, the idea should pick up, and people will begin phoning in on their own."

"Je trouve la cuisine française très tentante," the woman at the table behind her said. Brit felt her backbone hardening.

Eugenia leaned over and cupped her hand over her mouth. "She said she finds French food very tempting," she translated in a giggling whisper.

"I'll bet," Halbrook threw in with a grin, then winced when he saw he'd offended Brit again.

"Aimons-vous le vin?" Kitty asked Joe. Brit glanced over her shoulder and saw that an enchanted grin was slicing across Joe's face, ear to ear.

"Uh-oh." Eugenia propped her chin on her hand. "So much for fluent French."

"What?"

"She doesn't know how to conjugate her verbs. It's *aimez-vous*, not *aimons-vous*. Hope he doesn't give her a written test before the wedding."

Brit slammed her hand down. "I knew it! She's an impostor!"

Halbrook tried to cover his laughter with his napkin. "Mr. Dillon doesn't seem to notice."

"No, he doesn't," Eugenia agreed, great amusement dancing in her eyes. "Don't those people realize this used to be a church?"

Brit felt a fierce headache coming on and abruptly slid back her chair. "If you'll excuse me," she said briskly, "I need to freshen up. I'll be right back."

"Want me to come with you?" Eugenia whispered.

"No," Brit whispered harshly. "What I want is for you to be my agent, not another adoring fan of Joe Dillon. How about that?"

Eugenia made an unflattering face at her client, laughed knowingly and turned back to Mr. Halbrook.

The ladies' room at the converted abbey had a sitting room with large, lighted mirrors and velvet chairs on which Brit could sit and stare at her wan complexion and pale features. She dropped into a chair and shook her head dolefully. She looked awful. How could a woman who had been satisfied with her looks an hour ago feel like such a frump now?

She pulled out her brush and ran it through her hair. It was so light, she thought miserably. So blonde. She stuffed her brush back into her purse and pulled out her lipstick. What was the point? she asked herself as she began applying it. All it did was make her face look paler.

What in heaven's name was Joe trying to prove, anyway? she ranted fiercely, smacking her lips. That he could get to her? Or that he could forget her? If he expected her to believe that his showing up here was

pure coincidence, then he was crazy. He had probably followed her here.

Determined not to let her vexation show again, she
took a deep cleansing breath, stood up, and stepped
out of the bathroom. She paused in the lobby for another breath.

"Nervous?" a voice behind her asked.

She swung around to see Joe Dillon leaning next to
the door, arms crossed indolently over his chest,
looking for all the world like a man just trying to pass
the time outside the ladies' rest room. "What's the
matter, Joe? Isn't your search going well? Have you
given up the newspaper ads and taken to hanging out
at ladies' rooms?"

Joe seemed to enjoy her irritation. "I was waiting
for you," he admitted. "And you didn't answer my
question. You've seemed nervous ever since I walked
in. Is something wrong?"

"No," she snapped. "Everything's going very well
for me. *You* should be nervous, though. Cat Woman
acts as if she'll start tearing your clothes off any minute now. You should watch that, you know. I don't
believe they allow that in an establishment like this."

"Her name's Kitty," Joe said with an extremely
satisfied grin. "I wanted to catch you to see what you
thought of her."

Brit forced a mendacious smile, though she doubted
her face was pale anymore. It was probably glowing
like the alarm button on a nuclear warhead. "She's
perfect, Joe," she said caustically. "Snap her up."

"You don't like her," he said without the slightest hint of regret. "Why?"

Brit gave a false laugh and threw up her hands dramatically. "Why? I don't know, Joe. It certainly couldn't be because she pranced in here with her dress open to her navel, or that she smells like a bordello, or that she behaves like a nymphomaniac in a public place, or that she can't even conjugate her verbs!"

That maddening grin broadened across his face. "Conjugate her verbs! What are you talking about?"

"Her French, Mr. Impeccable Judgment. The woman doesn't even know how to conjugate her verbs, and you're seriously considering *marrying* her!"

Brit's vision blurred when he stumbled back, laughing at her without restraint, and she attributed the blur to the cloud of smoke originating in the vicinity of her ears.

"At least she knows a little French," he said finally, wiping the mist from his eyes. "That's more than you can say."

"If I were to take up French," Brit volleyed, "I'd sure as heck learn it right!"

"You flunked Spanish!" he reminded her. "How can you say that?"

So they had resorted to mudslinging, had they? she seethed. "Fine, Joe. Change the subject. If you want to marry an impostor, go ahead. Have a wonderful life! It just seems to me that I remember your griping about hating those safe little restaurant meetings, those getting-to-know-you conversations...."

"God, you're jealous! Your eyes are turning green! Look at you." He lifted a strand of her hair. "Even your hair is taking on a bit of a lime cast."

"Get your hands off me!" She slapped his hand down and moved away. "You're making me mad. I am not jealous. I just hate to see someone making such a herculean mistake."

"I haven't made any mistakes," Joe said, still grinning. "Matter of fact, everything's going just the way I planned it."

It didn't take a genius to know he was referring to Brit's reaction. She backed against the wall and closed her eyes, counting to ten, and found that her temper was still at a lethal level. "I knew it," she whispered furiously. "You followed me here, didn't you?"

"Followed you? Of course not. Don't be ridiculous." He slid his hands into his pockets and lifted his shoulders innocently. "I simply called Mr. Halbrook's secretary and told her I was your agent confirming our dinner date. I'm not without my resources, you know. I was a little amused by the choice of restaurants, though. An abbey? Somehow it seemed fitting when the business you're cooking up might as well lock you in one."

Her eyes flew open and she gulped when she saw Joe standing much too close, his elbow propped on the wall above her head. "You had no right to come here," she said.

"Did you get my French cassette?" he asked.

"Yes. Maybe I should pass it on to Pussy Cat—"

"Kitty," he interjected.

"Whatever. She seems to need it more than I do."

"You don't need it at all," he whispered, his eyes assessing her lips with great interest. "You excite me enough in English. I only sent it to let you know my foot is still in the door."

"Feet have been known to be crushed to smithereens," she warned. "Especially when they're in my door."

Brit looked up at him, felt the warmth of his chest close to hers, his knee brushing her thigh, his clean, unobtrusive scent making her dizzy. He wet his lips and her stomach took a dive. He was going to kiss her, right here in the lobby of the restaurant, with her agent and producer sitting in the next room and his hussy of a date waiting for him with her claws out. He was getting closer, and she could almost taste him, as well as the fear and apprehension rising inside her.

And there wasn't a thing in the world Brit could do about it.

He tasted of Dom Perignon and moist heat and shivering excitement. He felt like the drenching wash of an ocean wave that pulled her out and under, threatening until it let go at last and allowed her to catch her breath before it did its work again. He felt like the burn of an August wind, scorching inside and out, erasing all thoughts except for easing the ache....

He broke the kiss and looked down at her, no amusement left in his eyes. "What do you say if I take Kitty home and meet you back at your place in an hour?" he whispered.

She swallowed and pushed against his chest in vain. "No. That shouldn't have happened. It won't happen again." She tried to move away, but he caught her hand and moved it to his hammering heart.

"It'll happen again and again until you finally see what's best for you," he said.

"And what is that?" she asked. "A man who's achieved national notoriety for his high-profile search for a wife? I don't need that kind of publicity. And I don't want to be linked with you as one of your finalists."

"All or nothing?" he asked, undaunted. "Is that what you want?"

"No," she said. "*Nothing* or nothing. What I want is my syndicated television show, my seminars and to be left alone. Can you give me that?"

He gazed at her, breaking through the guarded glass shields over her soul, reading her in a way she could not read herself. "I don't know," he admitted quietly.

"Well, you can sure make me lose them. And if you have any respect for me at all, you won't do that."

His eyes narrowed seriously as he looked into hers, and for a moment Brit wondered if he'd found something she hadn't known was there. "Maybe I see you backing yourself into the same kind of corner I'm in," he whispered. "Maybe I'm trying to save you from yourself—the way you're trying to save me from the Kittys and the Russian spies and the impostors of the world."

"Why don't we stop trying to save each other from anything?" she asked. "Why don't we go back to our tables and forget that we're both here?"

"Why don't we go back to my place and forget we ever *were* here?"

Brit shook her head. The man was beyond hope. "I'm going to be in town at least six weeks, Joe, and longer if this show goes through. Don't make me afraid to go out for fear of running into you."

A vein in Joe's temple twitched, and a flash shot through those obsidian eyes. Joe dropped his hands to his sides in feigned resignation. "You're right," he said too quickly. "Our priorities are different. Our values are incompatible." He slid his hands into his pockets and glanced back toward the dining room. "So maybe Kitty isn't the right one. Maybe none of my applicants are. But I'll find her soon, and I'll marry her. And she'll make me forget the little blond spitfire who got under my skin and kept me awake nights."

"My producer's waiting for me," Brit whispered, her voice quivering. Something inside her quivered as well, when Joe dropped a kiss on her forehead and left her standing there alone.

"I'm not saying you should cloister yourself," Eugenia told her later that night as they sat in the hotel bar, discussing how the dinner had gone. "I'm just saying that Halbrook is almost ready to offer us a contract. We don't want some dead-end crush to spoil it all."

"Dead-end crush? What are you talking about?"

"Joe Dillon," Eugenia said, ennui lacing her voice. "It's getting pretty obvious to me, if no one else."

"I do not have a crush on Joe Dillon!"

Eugenia gave her an unconvinced look. "Oh, really? Is that why you both disappeared from your tables at the same time and came back almost twenty minutes later?"

Brit's face flushed as it had when she'd found Joe outside the rest room. "We were just talking. We ran into each other and . . ."

"Ran right into each other's mouths, huh?" Eugenia asked.

Brit stared at her, horrified.

"I came looking for you to see if you were all right. I saw that you were in good hands—literally—and went back to the table."

Mortified, Brit laid her face in her hands. "Good grief," she breathed. "Did Mr. Halbrook know?"

"No. But that isn't to say that your interest in Joe wasn't obvious to him, too."

She grabbed the defensive with both hands and met Eugenia's eyes. "You know, you didn't help matters any. Telling him I said Joe was gorgeous, when I didn't."

"Well, good Lord, I thought we were covered when he walked in with that woman. How was I to know you were going to go play kissy-face with him at the bathroom?"

"We were not playing kissy-face!" Brit grated.

"Well, that's beside the point. Halbrook doesn't have any solid evidence, and at the moment I think he's inclined to go ahead and try the show out. But you'll have to toe the line, Brit. One clue that things will go wrong and producers run like hell. I mean it. You'll have to quit Joe Dillon cold turkey. No more quick fixes by bathrooms."

Brit threw back her drink with the gusto of a sailor on leave, then stared at the glass, wishing she'd ordered something alcoholic. "You're making this sound so sleazy," she said. "I didn't plan it, you know. It just happened."

"It always just happens, Brit. That's how love is."

"Love!" Brit almost choked on the word. "Wait a minute. You've got the wrong idea here. You're way off."

"It isn't that I'm not happy that you finally got bitten," Eugenia said as if she hadn't even heard. "It's just that you couldn't have picked a worse time. An affair now could cost you your whole future."

"Read my lips, Eugenia. I am not having an affair. He is not some perverted kind of addiction. And most of all, I am not in love!"

"Good," Eugenia said. "Then I think we're home free. I think I can get Halbrook to agree to a test show by next week. Of course, I had to do quite a bit of finagling while you were supposedly in the bathroom. It was a stroke of genius...." She paused for effect, sipped her drink, and waited until Brit was sufficiently anxious.

"Eugenia! What?"

"I made him an offer he couldn't refuse. I offered him a clause in the contract that says you may not get married during the life of the show, and that any relationship deemed risky by the station will be broken off immediately. Halbrook loved it. Snapped it right up. You would have thought I'd offered him the Hope Diamond."

Brit's chin fell like lead, leaving her mouth gaping open while her eyes blazed blue flames. "You might as well have offered him the Hope Diamond," she said. "You had about as much right to give it."

"Come on, Brit," Eugenia soothed. "I was backed into a corner. I felt him losing interest, hemming and hawing around about how tight money is these days, how they weren't sure they wanted to commit—"

"But how could you offer him that? It's ridiculous, not to mention probably illegal!"

Eugenia looked genuinely insulted. "Well, what do you care? You never planned to get married. And personally, I think it would stand up in court, considering the nature of your show. It's really quite reasonable." She reached across the table and took Brit's hand, suddenly cold and clammy. "The show's yours for a very small price. It's all up to you, kiddo."

Brit stared at Eugenia's hand over hers as if it were the cuff that would bind her for life. She couldn't blame Eugenia, not when she'd talked of nothing else for months. Eugenia was doing her job, and no one was going to accuse Brit of being a whiner.

"I can handle it," Brit said quickly, suddenly feeling as if she'd just given her left foot for a shot at the

big time. She would get her show, thus fulfilling her
dreams and reaching her goals, but she'd limp for the
rest of her life! Was that having it all? Suddenly she
wasn't all that certain she wanted to "quit" Joe Dillon cold turkey, or sign away the options that made life
a challenge. But telling herself the club soda had gone
to her head, she snuffed out her rebellion and tried to
appear cooperative.

The drowning sensation she'd felt in Joe's arms in-
vaded Brit's dreams that night, pulling her under its
deadly current again, but this time it wasn't playful
like the waves. This time it threatened to wash the life
from her and send her floating, limp, downstream.
She groped for a lifeline, and suddenly one was thrown
to her. And then it wasn't a line at all, but a hand.
Joe's hand.

She sat up in bed, rigid and damp with perspiration, and gulped for breath. He wasn't the one
drowning her, she thought suddenly. It was the narrow boundaries of a career that threatened to smother
her now.

Maybe I'm trying to save you from yourself.

She pulled out of bed, walked to the bathroom and
splashed cold water on her face. What was happening
to her? A month ago she would have seen her ascend-
ing career as a wide-open field of possibilities . . . not
some kind of prison. But a month ago she hadn't
kissed Joe Dillon.

She looked in the mirror and wondered if she'd been as transparent with Joe tonight as she was right now. Had he seen that his kiss shook her right to her core? Had he felt her trembling in his arms?

She'll make me forget the little blond spitfire who got under my skin and kept me awake nights.

Was he awake now, thinking of her, wondering how she felt? Was he planning new ways to get under *her* skin? Or had he already found the one who could make him forget?

She went back to her bed, sat down on it and looked at the phone, lying mute in the darkness. If she could only hear his voice, she thought, maybe it would set him back in his rightful place as a mere annoyance in her life. Maybe the sheer reality of him would pop the bubble of fantasy he had started growing within her tonight.

She went to the dresser for the number he'd given her the morning he had come here and, with a trembling hand, dialed. What would she say? she asked herself. Would she just sit there like a fool? Would he think she was crazy?

She finished dialing and held her breath as the telephone rang. What if it was worse than that? she panicked. What if he was with that woman, and she answered the phone, and . . .

Before the phone could ring a third time, she slammed it down, unable to carry through. She was losing her mind, she thought miserably, burying her head in her pillow. At the rate she was going, she just might wind up in that padded room, after all.

Joe stared at the phone in his hand and frowned at the dial tone. The ringing had shaken him from an already shallow sleep. Who would be calling in the middle of the night, only to hang up before he even answered?

The answer came to him like a lightning bolt, and he sat up straight in bed. Brit. It had to be Brit.

He smiled in relief and pressed a kiss on the receiver. So she was thinking of him.

He thought of calling her back, of telling her that he wanted to hear her voice, too, that he wanted to come to her hotel and hold her, and make love to her, and wake up with her in the morning. But it would be too easy for her to hang up, and denial wasn't what he needed just now.

What he needed was Brit. And somehow, if it killed them both, Joe planned to have her.

Chapter Seven

At first, when she heard the light knock on her door, Brit thought she was dreaming. The music that had been drifting up through the hotel's atrium from the lobby diminished, and quiet was settling in for the night. The knock was probably at the room next door, she reasoned, if she'd indeed heard it at all.

But it came again, more distinct this time. She rolled over and looked at the clock, saw that it was 12:30. Alarmed, she got out of bed and grabbed her robe, holding it tightly around her like some measly protection. If it was some drunk who'd seen her come in here, she could handle him, she told herself. She'd spent plenty of time teaching self-defense techniques as part of her seminar. She knew just what to do. First she'd break his nose with the heel of her hand, then she'd twist his arm unmercifully. If she had to, she'd flip him a couple of times until she had him helpless and begging for mercy.

But the knock didn't seem threatening. It seemed almost tentative, as if it would stop momentarily if there were no answer. Quietly, she tiptoed to the door. "Who—who is it?" she asked.

"Joe."

His voice made her gasp, and she backed away from the door as if a fire from the other side made it too hot to touch. Joe! What was he doing here?

"Brit?"

Catching her breath and forcing herself to act normally—if that could be done when absolutely nothing had been normal in days—she fumbled to open the locks. When she cracked the door, she peered up at Joe, all rumpled and tired and leaning forlornly against her casing.

"Joe?" she asked.

"I couldn't sleep," he whispered. He slipped inside and closed the door behind him, assessing her terry robe and her tangled hair and her blue eyes bare of makeup. He'd never seen her look better.

"So you drove twenty miles for company?" she asked.

He shrugged and pulled his hands out of his windbreaker, palms up. "Hey, good company's hard to find. Besides, the cab driver didn't mind."

"I trust the meter's still running," she whispered, feeling more vulnerable than she'd ever felt in her life. If only he'd stop *looking* at her like that.

Joe shook his head. "I sent him on his merry way."

Something in Brit's throat constricted, and she tried to swallow. "What was wrong with Kitty's company?"

"Nothing," he said. "She was just fine. But there's a vital difference between you and her."

"Joe..."

He took her shoulders and gazed down into her eyes, and she felt her defenses drop like armor too heavy to support. "The vital difference is that you keep me awake nights, and keep me from concentrating on anything else, and drive me absolutely nuts. Now, what's a guy like me supposed to do about that?"

Her mouth suddenly felt like cotton. He felt so warm, so close, and she didn't want to step away, even if it meant relinquishing a little of herself.

"You know what happened about half an hour ago?" he rumbled, his voice growing huskier, breathier with each word. "I was lying in bed, almost asleep, and I was dreaming of you. And then the phone rang."

Brit refused to allow her face to incriminate her, so she struggled to keep any expression from it. "Who... who was it?" she whispered.

"Dial tone," he said. "Wrong number, I guess. But you know what my first crazy thought was?"

"What?" The word came out hoarse and broken.

"I thought it was you. And then I realized it was only wishful thinking, because you couldn't be lying awake thinking of me, too."

An electric moment of tension passed between them, long and sizzling. Her voice sounded small and far away when she asked, "So why did you come?"

"Because that thought just wouldn't leave my mind," he whispered, his minty breath sweeping her lips. "And I knew I wouldn't have any peace the rest of the night until I held you one more time."

The crystal composure in Brit's heart shattered as his lips descended to hers. Why did he feel so much like belonging when she didn't want to belong? Why did he feel like a commitment when she hadn't committed in years?

He coaxed her lips open and made a sweet exploration of her mouth. The shattered pieces of her heart melted like ice on July cement. Of their own accord, her hands slid up his back. His breathing quickened against her face, hot and sexy and maddening, as his tongue performed an ancient dance ritual against her own. His hands slid down the nylon of her robe to the slope of her back. The gentle pressure brought her seductively against him, hard and alive, tremblingly anxious to fulfill the deep burning need they both suffered.

His hair was black silk and satin threads, and she stood on her toes to touch it. The kiss deepened more when he slipped one side of her robe from her shoulder and she didn't object. The other was pushed aside, and the robe fell to the floor.

Brit's flesh burned against the thin nylon between them. His hard lower body moved against hers in a primitive rhythm, inciting a riot in the depths of her stomach. His mouth broke free of hers and fell to her neck, wet and sensual. One strap fell from her shoulder, and she wrapped her arms around his head as he followed its trail. Chests heaved, lungs strained, as he moved the other strap and let the top of her gown drop to bare her breasts.

His stubbled chin trailed down her chest, and he took one pink, straining mound in his mouth. Brit gasped, then exhaled in a long, quivering sigh. His rough, masculine hand kneaded the other, making her legs weak and her heart shudder. She dropped her mouth to his hair, burying her face in the clean, forest scent.

Suddenly, he brought his face back to hers and took her mouth again in a searing claim. A thin mist of perspiration erupted across her skin, and she felt the need to feel his bare chest against her breasts, heat against heat, male against female. Her fingers shivered as she opened his buttons one by one and slid his shirt off his arms. He was muscular perfection with a T-shaped line of dark hair that she ran her hands over in silent exploration. He moved her against him, nipples brushing nipples, and moaned gently into the kiss.

She felt him backing to the bed, pulling her with him, and when he lay back, she fell above him. Her soft hair made a blond veil around their faces as her breasts crushed into his chest. His breath came in shudders, and his hand lowered to gather the folds of her long gown, allowing him more freedom.

Before she knew what had happened, he had rolled her over and was above her, the hard lines of his clothed maleness rocking against her as his mouth played games in which her only source of breath was his, her only source of strength was him.

"I want you, Brit," he whispered against her mouth. "Not Kitty...not those eight thousand others. You...I want you.... And not just for tonight..."

The honesty in his voice broke the bubble of fantasy forming in her mind and shot right through to that special point between emotion and intellect, where the two mingled and were heard. "No," she whispered.

"Yes," he said. "You want me, too."

"Not forever," she whispered. "It can't be forever."

She felt his muscles growing tense, and he raised his head, his eyes pleading down at her. "It can't be just tonight," he said.

Tears stung her eyes as her mind struggled with the answer. What was she asking? That it be a one-night stand? She didn't want that any more than she did a lifetime commitment. But with Joe, could there be a middle ground? Wasn't it one or the other?

Reality blazed through the darkness in her mind—reality in the form of a contract that said she could have the moon, the stars and the heavens—but never Joe Dillon. "Then it can't be," she whispered.

She felt him stiffening above her, holding his breath as his eyes sought an ally somewhere in her heart. When he found none, he sat up, his tanned back rippling in the lamp light as he ground his elbows in his knees and laid his forehead on his hands. "What is it with you?" he asked quietly.

Brit quickly pulled her gown up and slipped her arms back through the straps. A tear dropped onto the pink nylon, and she wiped it away before he could see. The emotion clogging her throat kept her from answering.

"I can tell you react to me. Every time I've touched you—"

"I don't let myself be ruled by my hormones, Joe. I'm stronger than that."

He turned around to her, sitting like a rumpled goddess on the bed, still flushed from his love. "There are other things besides hormones, Brit." He trailed his finger down her neck and stopped over her heart. "There's something a lot more important."

She wondered if he felt her pulse lurch against his finger, testifying that she did have a heart that ached and yearned and broke. "But I have my whole life to think of," she whispered. "Just being seen with you could hurt me in big ways. What if you knew that being with me could make your whole electronics company collapse?"

"I guess I'd have to think real hard about it. But my company doesn't keep me warm at night, and my company can't talk to me, and laugh with me and give me children...."

Incipient tears sparkled in her eyes. "So you think I should just risk my whole career for a man I've known a few days? Become a laughingstock when the press links us together and I become another statistic for your stupid computer?''

"Laughingstock? What are you talking about?''

"I'm talking about the poor women you've been taking out on these ridiculous 'interview dates.' Don't you realize they're setting themselves up to be ridiculed? Don't you care? I wouldn't be caught dead with you if I thought some sleazy reporter might think I was competing to be your wife! It would ruin me in more ways than one.''

Joe stood up, anger rampant on his face. "So it's your image you're worried about. Forget feelings, forget attraction, just don't threaten that lily-white image of yours.''

"That isn't fair!'' she said. "You know what's on the line here. This show I'm working for is the main reason I scheduled seminars in Atlanta in the first place. Not to meet men. If I get this show, I have to sign a contract that says I can't get married, and I can't get involved with anyone seriously for the life of the show. If that doesn't bring it down to an either-or choice, I don't know what does.''

His face twisted in disbelief. "You can't sign that!'' he shouted. "It's primitive. There are laws against contracts like that!''

"I'm not so sure,'' Brit volleyed. "Eugenia thinks the nature of my show justifies it, and I don't plan to find out in court. If it's the only way I can get the show, I'll sign it.''

"It could ruin your life!'' he bellowed.

"Not if I don't let it," she said. "And I'll make a confession, if you want me to. That first day we met, in that stupid college confrontation, you said that finding Mr. Right would mean ruining my credibility and my career and that it would reduce me to a woman who wants marriage, two-point-five kids and a station wagon. Well, as much as I objected, you were right."

"Then you're admitting that I'm Mr. Right?"

"No! You couldn't be more *wrong*! My career doesn't prohibit me from seeing men, or even getting involved with them, as long as my producers don't consider it too serious. But you...you're parading around letting everyone know how desperate you are for a wife. Anyone seen with you is an automatic candidate. Getting involved with you isn't like being linked with someone else. It's like instant engagement. And the very idea that I would be in the running destroys the whole premise for my show."

"So does that contract!" he said. "Letting them manipulate your love life...Halbrook didn't have to sign any crock like that. If you were a man, they wouldn't ask it. You're teaching women to be equal and independent while you compromise and submit all over the place. *That* goes against the premise of your show, Brit." Joe grabbed his shirt from the floor and shrugged it on. "Let me get this straight. If I were some ordinary guy, some confirmed bachelor who treated women like they were bedsheets that needed to be changed every couple of days, you'd get involved?"

"No, that's not what I meant. But there is a middle ground somewhere. I'm not asking you to give up your goals, the things that are important to you. How can you ask *me* to?"

"*They're* asking that, not me! I just asked for you to care about me for more than one night."

"That, in itself, is a death warrant for my career."

Joe buttoned his shirt and tucked it in his pants, his face a vicious shade of red. "Well, it looks like you've just got it all figured out, haven't you?"

"No. I just know what's best for me."

"You don't know what's best for you. You just know what you've brainwashed yourself into believing."

There seemed to be nothing more to say, so they only stared at each other across the dim room. Finally, Joe raked his hands through his hair and headed for the door, slamming it behind him.

Brit thought she must have stared at that door for fifteen minutes or more before she locked it and went back to bed. But there was no chance of sleep tonight.

The cab ride home seemed to last forever, and Joe stared out the windows into the black Atlanta night speckled with colored lights. It wasn't supposed to happen this way, he told himself over and over. When he'd decided that marriage was what he wanted, he'd expected the choice to be systematic, ordered and fairly easy. He'd expected to make that choice, set the date, tie the knot and live happily ever after. And then he'd met Brit.

He rubbed his weary face and laid his head back on the dirty vinyl seat. He'd built an empire from one small electronics store that had multiplied into thousands. He'd invested his fortune and watched it grow a hundredfold. He'd scraped his way from being known as wealthy Arnold Dillon's oldest son to being Joseph Dillon, of Dillon Electronics, where people from Chunky, Mississippi, to Alice, North Dakota, shopped for batteries and computers, stereos and telephones, robots and VCRs. He'd done things they'd said could not be done.

But he couldn't make Brit Alexander love him.

Defeatism was foreign to him, and not fond of its fit, Joe Dillon shrugged it off. To hell with giving up, he thought. He hadn't gotten where he was by accepting defeat. In the past, if he didn't know the game, he learned it. Then he knew how to compete.

So Brit had chosen her seminars and television show over a relationship with him. Maybe it was time he learned just why they were so important to her. Maybe it was time he checked out his competition, so he'd have a better idea of how to fight it.

A wry grin dawned across his weary face as the idea came to him, stark against the rejection growing dimmer by the moment.

Brit's seminar students filed into her classroom the following Saturday, eager to absorb her teachings about improving their lives. She checked registration cards as they came in, making certain that the students had registered and were in the right class. When the room seemed to be full, she went back to her desk to begin the seminar.

A feeling of purpose stole over her as her eyes swept over the room, over the faces of women who were tired of being victims, women who knew there was a better way and intended to find it, women who acted to change their lives instead of complaining about it. She could help them all, she knew, for she had what they needed.

She smiled, a smile that was neither superior nor condescending, but a kinship smile, for she knew what had brought them here. It was more than gratifying when they smiled back. Lana Bell, sitting in the back row, smiled more than the rest, almost self-consciously, as if she didn't quite know why she was here.

"You're all here for a reason," Brit said, her voice carrying throughout the lecture hall. "You all want to improve your life. You all want more self-esteem. You all want more respect. You all want a number of other things. I promise to give those to you by the time you finish this class." She swept her eyes over the class, evaluating the varying styles of dress, the differing hairstyles, the combinations of defiance and humility.

Brit singled out a woman in the front row who wore a stiff blazer with football-quality shoulder pads. "Could you tell me why you're here?" she asked.

"Because I'm tired of having to act like a man to get my job done," the woman said gruffly.

Brit nodded and found another face, one that looked nervous and jumpy. "And you?"

"I'm just divorced," the woman said in a strained voice. "I just need some . . . reinforcements. Something to make me feel better than I am."

"Better than you are, or better than you've been made to feel like you are?"

The woman breathed a defeated laugh and shrugged.

"You've come to the right place," Brit assured her. She looked around the room at other faces, and her eyes rested on one that seemed even more eager than the others. "Why are you here?" she asked the pixieish girl in the center of the class.

"To find out how to get along without men," the young woman blurted frankly. "I decided to try to readjust my thinking so that I can live my life with some sort of permanency, instead of thinking it's only a temporary condition until some bozo sweeps me off my feet."

A round of applause erupted over the audience, complete with shouts of approval. Brit laughed aloud at the relaxing feeling blossoming as the students loosened up. The door at the back of the class opened, and she glanced toward it as the applause continued. The smile froze on her face.

Joe Dillon and his hopeless cohort, Jerome, stepped inside.

Immediately, the applause ceased, and every head turned to the door. Joe grinned with cocky indifference, gave a little salute and dropped into a chair in the back row. Jerome slipped in past him and slumped next to him.

"I'm sorry," Brit said through her teeth. "But this is a seminar for women. I don't allow visitors."

"We're not visitors," Joe said. "We both registered. Wanna check our cards?"

"*I* registered the students myself," Brit informed him. "I didn't register you."

Lana Bell cleared her throat and slid upright in her seat. "Uh, Brit?" she drawled timidly. "I'm afraid I might of . . . um, signed them up, a few days after registration. I thought they were registering their wives . . . or sisters . . . or something."

Jerome winked at Lana Bell, and she blushed too obviously.

"*Anybody* who reads the paper knows I'm not married," Joe said.

A few chuckles drifted over the class, testimony that the women, indeed, recognized the notorious man.

"Besides, isn't there some law against sex discrimination?" he went on.

Brit wondered if anyone had ever lost the top of their head strictly from a burst of blood pressure. He was undermining her, and she wouldn't forgive him. If she couldn't talk him out, she could at least make sure he didn't cause a scene that could ultimately rob her of credibility.

"I say we let Mr. Dillon stay," Brit suggested to the class, surprising him. "I don't think it would hurt him to learn a few lessons about women. After all, he's the perfect example of what we're having to fight against."

The class murmured approval. Ignoring the two men at the back of the room, Brit went on about her business as if they weren't there.

Well, well, Joe thought a little while later. The lady knew her stuff. He'd taken scores of notes and heard horror stories from these women about discrimination, harassment and manipulation due to their sex. Brit had answers. Good ones. And she was giving these women something that no one else had been able to give them. She was giving them hope. And choices.

But damn it all, she was ignoring him completely, as if he weren't even here. He had come to see what she was about, but in the back of his mind he'd also hoped to shake her up a little, remind her that he was still alive, that the rejection in her hotel room the other night may have cooled him off, but it hadn't snuffed out his feelings completely. His foot was still in the door.

Instead, she was shaking *him* up. He wanted to lash out, tell her to notice him, to pay him some attention, to slip in some sign that he was getting to her. But there was no crack in her facade and no stumbling in the well-ordered lessons she taught.

When class had been in session two hours, she allowed them a fifteen-minute break. Joe stood up thankfully, ready to make his move. But Brit only strutted past him without meeting his eye.

Damn that woman! he thought. Maybe it was time to fight fire with fire. Maybe it was time for Plan B.

Brit fumed in the rest room, struggling to regain her feigned composure. What was he *doing* here? What did he want?

At first she had been certain he was out to destroy her, except that he hadn't argued, and had asked only pertinent questions, occasionally provided the male side to a woman's problem that arose and taken notes as diligently as any other student in the class. Never mind that Jerome had distracted Lana Bell beyond repair. He wasn't her problem. But Joe was.

Maybe he really did want to learn what she was trying to teach, she thought. Maybe he deserved more than her first conclusion this morning. Maybe she was being unfair.

She took a deep, cleansing breath and decided to go back out there and be cordial. Hostility wasn't her best suit, and it kept her from liking herself very much.

Straightening her hair and dress, she pushed through the door and out into the hall. All thoughts of cordiality fled her mind as she saw Joe laughing in the hall, surrounded by five flirting women who obviously had heard nothing she'd said all morning.

"Mr. Dillon, may I have a word with you?" she asked in a carefully controlled voice.

He cast her an indifferent look through the women. "Sure, no problem. You ladies don't mind, do you?"

Brit seethed as the women reluctantly went back into the class room. "Bottom line," she said, hands on hips. "What are you trying to prove?"

"Nothing," he said. "Not one thing."

"Then what did you come here for? To pick up girls?"

A flash of anger passed over his face, but he quickly recovered his unaffected, saccharine grin. "You guessed it," he said. "I figured what better place to find a woman than a seminar like this?"

"You're despicable."

"And you're predictable," he said, eyes blanching. "Somehow I knew you'd find some sleazy intention in my coming here. Couldn't you consider for one minute that I may want to hear what it is you're about? Why your career is more important than your feelings? Whether or not it's worth it?"

"You could take my word for it," she said, her anger softening a little.

"No, ma'am, I can't. I paid my money and I'm gonna hear you out. And if I run into the perfect candidate for a wife while I'm here, then I'll just chalk it up to fate."

Before Brit could respond, he was back inside, in his seat, studying his notes as if expecting a pop quiz.

Somehow, Brit felt as if she had already been tested and failed. Still, as she marched past him, she couldn't resist bending down and warning, "You'd better not embarrass me, Joe. I'll never forgive you if you do."

A mute salute was all the reply he offered.

* * *

It was after five when the segment of her seminar called "Myth and the American Dream" had wound down and all her students' questions had been answered. Giving them a personal assignment for the next day, she dismissed them, then busied herself at her desk, bracing herself for the moment Joe approached her, for she knew he would.

She heard the room clearing out, heard Lana Bell's flirtatious laughter in the hall with Jerome, heard the familiar sound of emptiness minus one. And as she started to turn around, she felt his presence behind her, warm and imposing and entirely too magnetic.

"See?" he whispered. "I'm not so bad. I asked intelligent questions and I didn't embarrass you once, did I?"

She turned around and looked up at him, his face hovering much too close to hers. "Somehow, when I designed the segment called 'Social Life Without Singles' Bars,' I never thought my seminar would pave the way for some man to snag a wife."

He ignored the barb. "My favorite part was the self-defense," he said with a smile that curled her toenails. "I must have held my hand up for twenty minutes to be a volunteer. Guess you didn't see it."

She tried not to answer that smile. "I saw it. I didn't think it was wise to encourage you."

"I could have been the male dummy," he said. "They all could have worked their frustrations out on me. You know, the way you always do."

They grinned grudgingly at one another for a moment, their earlier hostility gone. As if it were second nature, Joe brought his hand up and brushed his knuckles across her cheek. "You know, this really is a great seminar. It's no wonder you're such a success."

"Thank you," she said.

"But you're more a women's advocate than a singles' advocate. All kinds of women could benefit from this."

"But I've created my career for singles," she said. "Anyone can come to the seminars, but primarily, that's what I stand for."

Joe nodded quietly and dropped his eyes to his fingers as they settled on her shoulder. A sizzling moment passed between them before he finally broke the tension. "I'm sorry about the other night," he whispered. "I have no right to come charging into your life demanding things. I'm really sorry."

"It's okay," she whispered, confusion rushing over her.

"No, it's not okay. I've put a lot of my life into my own career. I'd fight like hell, too, if anyone tried to destroy it. But there are other things in life, Brit. Some things a lot more important than how we make a living. It took me a long time, but I've learned the hard way."

His words held the ring of wisdom, and from some level far inside, she knew he was right. The school was suddenly quiet, suspended somehow, and it seemed as if the two of them were the only two left on the planet, on that tiny plateau of sanity they had found.

Slowly, his mouth lowered to hers, and even as she told herself that she should turn away, she found herself rising on her toes to meet him. The kiss was sweet as summer rain, gentle as a cool breeze, fresh as morning. It renewed the strength in her heart, as well as the ache that throbbed at odd times since she'd met him.

Suddenly a light flashed in her eyes, and she opened them to see a photographer standing at the door, intent on getting the picture of Joe Dillon's latest "interview." They sprang apart with a simultaneous gasp, and Brit's heart plopped to her toes. The sight of the man with the camera threw her with as much impact as the sight of the entire Midwest crumbling into some black hole might have.

"You son of a—" Joe dashed toward the man before Brit had time to move and grabbed his camera away from him. Flinging it onto a desk, he grabbed the man's collar and slung him against the wall. "If you print one word about what you just saw," he muttered through his teeth, "so help me God, I'll make sure you never have the breath left to report another friggin' thing. Understood?"

The man gaped up at him, red-faced and frightened. "Sure, man. Just give me the camera, how 'bout it? It's expensive."

Joe let him go with a violent thrust and picked up the camera. Viciously, he opened the back and pulled out the film, exposing it to the light.

"Hey, man! I had a three-car pileup on that roll. What am I gonna tell my editor?"

"Tell him you had the choice of surrendering your consciousness or your film," Joe said.

"I didn't do nothin'! One of the students here called the paper. I was just doing my assignment."

"Well, tell your editor any more assignments on me and I'll pull my company's ads so fast he won't have time to say 'bankruptcy.' Got that?"

"Yes, sir, I'll tell him. But you can't blame us. We thought you *wanted* publicity."

The photographer stumbled from the room, and Joe turned back to Brit, still holding the unrolled film in his hand, his shoulders heaving in fury. "I'm sorry, Brit," he said. "I guess you're right. Just being around me is instant trouble for you. This damned wife-hunt . . ."

His words broke off, and he swore under his breath.

Brit stepped toward him, gratitude in her eyes. "Thank you, Joe."

"Don't thank me," he said. "Not for making it easy for you to sign your future away. Not for carving you a door to slip away from me. And especially, not for hiding the fact that it's you I really want."

He flung the film into the trash, and it clicked against the metal. He started to leave the room, his lips held in a compressed line, but he turned back to her at the last moment.

"You know, Brit, if I had one hint that you cared for me—*one hint*—I'd reshoot that film myself and plaster it in every paper from here to L.A. I wouldn't walk out this door and let you forget I was ever here.

And I'd sure as hell make sure that dotted line was never there for you to sign on!''

Brit groped for an answer, but Joe didn't wait. Instead, he blew through the door like a tornado with damage yet to do.

Chapter Eight

Joe straightened the coat of his black suit and glanced toward the press room of Dillon Electronics' headquarters, where reporters were crowding into the room with the enthusiasm of the press when the president makes a major blunder. Joe only hoped that what he was about to do couldn't be classified as that. He turned back to Jerome, who leaned back against a boardroom table, arms crossed and biceps bulging. "So how do I look?" Joe asked.

"Oh-ay," Jerome said. "Like a million bucks."

"I'd *give* a million bucks to undo this mess."

"Hey, I told you, buddy. You let it out that you want a wife, you're sure to get yourself in trouble."

Joe went to the gilded mirror on the wall and straightened his tie. Somehow it felt like a noose around his neck. "Well, I'm about to get out of it. Right now."

"Hope it don't backfire," Jerome muttered.

Joe issued a heavy sigh and turned back to his friend. "You know me, man. I always land on my feet."

"But it ain't just you this time," Jerome pointed out.

Joe studied the floor for a moment. Yes, it was a risk. But he'd taken risks before. And he had to give it his best shot, because he hated like hell being depressed and doing nothing about it. It wasn't his style. Finally he looked squarely at the friend who seemed to have turned into his conscience. "I know what I'm doing."

Joe held out his palm and Jerome slapped it. "Break a leg, man."

"This isn't theater," Joe reminded him.

"Might as well be," Jerome chuckled.

Joe sucked in a deep breath that drew power and purpose into his posture. He opened the door and stepped into the room, immediately setting off an explosion of flashing cameras and shouted questions. Ignoring the hoopla, Joe walked to the podium and waited for quiet to settle. Slowly, the noise died down until the room got so quiet that he could hear his heart beating. He cleared his throat.

"I called this press conference today to announce that my search for a wife has come to an end—"

"Who is she!" several reporters shouted from various points in the room, and lights began flashing again.

"I'm not ready to give you a name," he said over the noise.

"Have you chosen her yet?" one reporter shouted. "Or is this just because you have enough applicants?"

Joe thought for a moment, then flashed the reporters a grin that would be plastered all over the papers the next morning, as well as the six o'clock news that night. "I've chosen her," he assured the reporters.

"What's she like?"

"What languages does she speak?"

"Is she someone you've been seen with in public?"

"She's dynamite," Joe assured them. "And yes, I may have been seen with her a time or two."

"When's the wedding?"

"We don't have a date yet, but you'll be the first to know," Joe assured them. Then, ignoring shouts of "When can you tell us her name?" and "Could you give us her initials?" he left the room smiling.

"What do you think?" he asked Jerome when he was safe in the boardroom again.

Jerome flashed him an approving thumbs-up sign. "I say we take the show to Broadway."

Brit was exhausted after the second day of her seminar, and she lay on her hotel bed in her bathrobe, eating room-service dinner and watching TV. Joe hadn't been in class that day, and she couldn't help watching the door, expecting him to pop in at any moment.

His knight-in-shining-armor stunt last night with that obnoxious photographer had proven to her that he really didn't want to embarrass her, just as she had proven a point to him with her seminar. In a way, they had earned each other's respect, even though Joe had left on an angry note. *One hint,* he'd said, and he'd pursue her until he caught her. She smiled slightly, thankful he didn't consider the way she had melted in his arms a hint. Brit realized her safest bet from now on was to stay as far away from him as she could, to avoid giving him that hint. But that didn't help the hungry craving in her heart and the disappointment she'd wrestled with all day when he'd skipped the seminar. She couldn't have a relationship with him, but on the other hand . . .

She sighed as the WTBS news rambled about a citizens' march in Atlanta today, but she couldn't have been less interested. A thought was taking shape in her mind, a thought of a secret relationship in which she could have Joe and her career, too. . . . It would be tough convincing him—maybe impossible—but what else could they do?

Her thoughts halted in midstream as Joe's face filled the television screen, and she sat up rigidly and groped for the remote control to turn it up.

" . . . when the popular bachelor took Atlanta by storm and announced his no-holds-barred search for a wife. Today that search came to an end when Joseph Dillon, electronics tycoon, announced that he has found a wife.''

Brit's mouth fell open and a queasy feeling gripped her as the camera zoomed in on Joe standing at the podium, grinning like a mischievous kid. ''She's dynamite,'' he was saying. ''And yes, I may have been seen with her a time or two.''

Kitty! Brit thought sickly. Or one of those other fakes! He was really going to do it!

The newswoman turned to her co-anchor. ''Who do you think it is, John?''

''It's hard to say,'' John returned, as if it were part of the script. ''He's been seen with quite a few. I wouldn't be surprised if bets were changing hands all over the country.''

The newswoman smiled into the camera, addressing the viewers. ''Well, in the interest of keeping it all fun, our station manager has instigated a game show that we'll be running between commercials. We'll have pictures of all of Joe Dillon's favorites. Call in if you think you know which one he chose, along with the wedding date, and if you're right, you could win $500.''

Brit slammed off the power button on the remote control and fell back onto the bed, staring in horror up at the ceiling. He was going through with it, for heaven's sake, in spite of everything he'd said. He was really going to do it!

Joe shook his garbage bag full of applications and photographs and walked slowly around his study, tearing down the beautiful faces of women he no longer wanted to know. Jerome came in from carting out the first few boxes full, and gasped as Joe reached for a half-naked beauty blowing kisses at the camera.

"Wait, man! Can I have that one?"

"Sure." Joe handed him the picture and started to tear another one down.

"I'll take that one, too," Jerome said. "And that one."

Joe grinned over his shoulder at him. "Phone numbers are on the back. Want their panties, too?"

"Then you *will* be redecorating your bedroom walls?" Jerome chuckled.

"Not funny," Joe said. "You're starting to sound just like her. Here, take all of them if you want them. I don't have any use for them anymore."

Joe leaned back on the desk that was clear for the first time in months and watched as Jerome ran around pulling down his favorites with the same gusto as a kid turned loose with a thousand dollars in a toy store.

The phone rang behind him, and idly he picked it up. "Joe Dillon," he said.

"So you're going to do it," Brit said. "You're really going to do it."

Joe grinned, motioning to Jerome that it was Brit, and lowered to his leather chair, innocence all over his face. "Yeah, I decided there was not much use in dragging this thing out. I figured I'd just go ahead and choose."

"I can't believe it!" she said, a slight quiver in her voice. "Which one is it? That dancer? Or the one with the mole on her upper lip? Is it Kitty?"

"I'm not ready to tell," he said smoothly.

"But you can tell *me*! I helped you narrow it down!"

"Narrow it down? You tried to convince me there wasn't one decent person in the whole batch."

"Well, I may have been right!"

Joe waited calmly for a moment, rubbing his grin. He winked at Jerome. "You know, this doesn't have to affect our friendship. I still like you a lot, and I hope we can go on talking to each other...."

"You've got a lot of nerve, you know that?" Brit blurted. Suddenly the call cut off with a ringing *click*, and Joe threw his head back and laughed harder than he had in weeks.

Brit had two days off to prepare for her next lecture at Oglethorpe University as well as prepare several possible formats for her show, but she made little headway in her work. Instead she sat glued to her television set, waiting for each installment of the Dillon's Choice Game Show in which three or four of his possibilities were featured, with the "call-in" number flashing across the screen like a notice that the world was ending. Somehow she felt that it was.

She almost forgot her appointment with Mr. Halbrook at the television station, and when she arrived her mind was a million miles away. But Mr. Halbrook was in better spirits than she'd ever seen him.

"I can't tell you how happy I was to hear that that man had finally chosen a wife," Halbrook said as he bustled around the studio.

"What man?" Brit asked obstinately.

"Joe Dillon, of course. I feel I should tell you that I was having serious reservations about your doing this show, even with the extra clauses in the contract, because I'd gotten very specific impressions that you were attracted to him."

"*Attracted?* You've got to be kidding."

"Not at all." Halbrook chuckled as if the idea had been foolish. "You just seemed so distracted the other night at the restaurant...."

"Well, if I was, it's because I find the whole idea of this wife-hunt appalling. I think it's degrading to women and it goes against everything I teach."

"That's understandable, I suppose," Halbrook said, "although our station is having a field day with this game show. It's boosted ratings tremendously already. I just hope he holds out a little while longer before releasing the name. We intend to milk this for everything it's worth."

Fury like white-hot lava flashed in her eyes. Was he serious? The man who insisted she sign away her right to marriage or love or any kind of commitment at all? The man who had the power to crush her if there was any clue that Joe wanted her? Now he was using the hunt to make a buck? She honestly wanted to scream. Her nostrils flared, but she forced them to relax. She would not let this upset her anymore. She *would not* let it threaten her! Forcing her thoughts back to the show that she reminded herself she wanted more than anything, she followed Halbrook into his office and began laying out her possible formats for the first show.

Later, exhausted but with little hope of getting any sleep tonight, since she didn't feel any less agitated than she had the night before, Brit drove back to the hotel, telling herself she needed to eat. But that queasy, helpless feeling hadn't left her stomach all day, and food only made her feel more defeated.

She wondered what the woman looked like. Was she one Brit had seen or a new entrant? She had luscious brown hair, no doubt. They all did. And she probably spoke French like a pro. And she probably had legs like a Rockette and flaunted them in her picture, and voluptuous curves in all the right places. She probably had Joe completely duped.

Tears stung her eyes, and she blinked them back as she waited for traffic to clear enough to pull into the parking lot. But instead of watching the traffic, she found herself staring into the smiling billboard-sized eyes of Joseph Dillon. "Uncle Joe Wants *You.*"

A fat, hot, furious tear plopped onto her cheek, and she slapped it away, unable to turn into the parking lot just yet. What was wrong with her? Why was this upsetting her so?

It was because she cared about him, she told herself. He was her friend, and she couldn't stand watching her friend make such a mammoth mistake. Yes, that was it. But what was she supposed to do? Storm over there and demand that he stop it? She had no more right to do that than he had when he demanded to be a part of her life.

As she'd told him earlier, he'd made his bed, now he had to sleep in it.

This morning I made your bed. Can I sleep in it?

That ridiculous rejoinder was the perfect example, she thought miserably. He wasn't ready for marriage. He didn't even know what he was doing.

Wearily, she pulled into the parking lot, got out of the car and scuffed to the hotel entrance. She felt like a little girl who hadn't made the cheerleading squad. But she hadn't been in the running! she told herself. Not for cheerleader, or wife, or anything!

She entered the lobby and stepped into the glass elevator that took her to her floor. She didn't know why she cared. If he wanted to ruin his life, he could have at it. It wasn't her problem.

She went to her room and kicked off her shoes. Disregarding the periwinkle-blue business dress she wore, she fell onto the bed and flicked on the television with the remote control.

The dreaded game show flashed on, complete with more pictures of women Joe had been seen with and more bits of information about each one. Her eyes ached with fury again, and when the phone rang, she jerked up the receiver. "Hello!"

"Brit? Honey, is that you?"

Brit sighed deeply and tempered her voice. "Yes, Mother. You just caught me at a bad time."

"Well, I won't keep you long. I was just wondering if you had any idea who that Joe Dillon man had picked for a wife. I thought I might enter that contest.''

"Mother, you're in *Boston*! How could you know about that?''

"It's cable, dear. Everybody watches it. You know him, don't you? Has he told you?''

Brit's teeth seemed to be grinding shorter by the moment. "No, Mother. Your guess is as good as mine.''

"But didn't you say you were helping him narrow down his choices?''

"I quit,'' she bit out. "It made me too angry.''

"Well, for heaven's sake, Brit. I could have won five hundred dollars if it weren't for your silly principles.'' Her mother paused. "Well, I guess I'll go with that Priscilla What's-her-name. Says she's a liaison for the foreign fashion industry and speaks three foreign languages. And she's so pretty. He probably picked her, don't you think?''

"Go for it, Mom!'' Brit shouted. "And good luck!'' She slammed down the phone and lay back on the bed, glaring at the ceiling.

She needed a shrink, that was what she needed. Someone who could tell her why she was turning into a basket case over this.

The news came on, and the anchor's headline story was that it was rumored that Joe Dillon would be making an announcement tomorrow, so the viewers had better get their guesses in to the station because it might be their last chance.

Brit threw the remote control against the wall.
"That does it!" she shouted. "He's got to be
stopped!"

Then, dragging on her shoes, she stormed out of her
room and back to her car, praying that he wouldn't be
there with his betrothed when she finally reached his
house.

The house seemed dark, but Brit could see a light
deep inside, probably in a room at the back of the
house. Forcing her heartbeat and breathing to slow,
she prayed that it wasn't the bedroom and that he
didn't have company.

Reminding herself she was here for a good cause,
she knocked firmly on the door. She waited a moment, then pressed the doorbell. The rough-and-
tumble melody of *Rawhide* played throughout the
house.

When Joe opened the door, Brit gaped up at him,
suddenly speechless. Why had she come? She honestly couldn't remember. All that was clear to her was
the surprise in his eyes and his male scent and the
warmth he emanated from his flannel shirt to the bare
feet beneath his jeans. Two words echoed in her mind
like a nightmarish admonition. *One hint...one hint...*
But his warning seemed no longer to apply.

"Brit," he said. "I didn't expect . . . come in."

"Are...are you alone?" she asked, wondering why
her voice suddenly refused to function reasonably. She
glanced past him, saw with relief that the light was on
in the kitchen, not the bedroom.

"Yes," he said quietly. "Come in." He closed the door and turned on the foyer light, casting her in a warm hue. "You look nice."

Brit glanced self-consciously down at her dress. "Thank you . . . I had a meeting . . . haven't changed." She caught her rambling and looked up at him, no longer able to play games. "Oh, Joe, I've been watching this ridiculous game show on television, and then tonight they said you were making an announcement tomorrow. I had to come over and talk some sense into you. You don't know what you're doing!"

Joe chuckled softly. "I assure you, Brit. I know exactly what I'm doing." He started back to the kitchen, and she followed, intent on making her point.

"No, you don't, Joe! You're making the mistake of your life!"

"Want some soup?" he asked, as if she'd just commented on the weather. "It's homemade."

"No," she said, though her stomach rebelled, reminding her that she hadn't eaten. "I came here to help you. As a friend."

"Can't friends share a pot of soup?" he asked. "You know, I hate to eat alone. That's one of the reasons I started this whole search to begin with."

"All right, I'll eat with you," she said. "Just to prove that you don't have to be married to enjoy a meal."

Joe smiled wryly and ladled her a bowlful. He handed her the bowl and a glass of grape Kool-Aid in a Wilma Flintstone glass, and sat down across from her, still smiling as if he had a secret.

Brit sampled it to quiet her wobbling stomach. "It's heavenly," she whispered. "I didn't know I was so hungry."

"And you think *I* need a keeper," he commented.

She set down the spoon and shot him a beseeching look. "Joe, can't you reconsider? Postpone this a few more weeks? Make sure?"

"I am sure," he said matter-of-factly. He unwrapped a roll of French bread and tore off a piece, then handed her the rest. "Want some?"

Brit grabbed a piece and took a bite. "I mean it, Joe. What's the rush? Why do you have to announce it tomorrow?"

"Why not? Why waste time?"

"Because!"

"Because? That's it?"

Brit sighed and dug into the soup again. "What does Jerome think about all this?" she asked after a moment.

"He's thrilled," Joe said. "He got to keep all my pictures. He figures his love life won't slow down for ten years or more. 'Course, he *says* he likes all my brunettes, but he sure didn't waste any time asking out that little red-haired friend of yours."

"Lana Bell?" Brit asked. "Did he really?"

"Yeah. They're going out after he does Hamlet Thursday night. She's coming to the show."

"Great," Brit said, feeling things growing worse the harder she tried to make them right. "I let her into the seminar free, and does she learn anything? No. She finds another man."

"What difference does it make to you?"

"A big difference. I don't like to see my friends making mistakes."

Joe folded his arms on the table and gave her a smile that was both sadness and entreaty, but he didn't say a word. Uneasy at his solemn expression, she set down her spoon, pulled out of her chair and strolled around the kitchen, wondering at the peculiar twist in her heart. Copper pots hung from low-hanging rafters overhead, and a big center island with a sink smelled of the spices and vegetables Joe had used in the soup.

She strolled back to the table and gazed out the big bay window overlooking the pond behind his house. "You have so much, Joe," she whispered. "I hate to see you lose it."

"I have nothing to lose," he said. "Only something to gain. I want a family, Brit."

She slid her fingers up through her hair and clutched her head dramatically. "How can I make you understand that you're wrong! I *am* your friend, and I can't stand to sit here and watch you tie yourself to some...some airhead who probably lied on her résumé and dyed her hair brown!" She turned back to him, pointing a shaking finger. "Did you make her speak to you in a foreign language? Did you *taste* her brownies?"

"If I said yes...?"

"It wouldn't matter!" she shouted, leaning over the table to make her point more clearly. "You can't speak another language yourself! How would you know she wasn't spouting off some nonsense sounds just to impress you? And *everybody* knows a brownie is a brownie! There aren't all that many variations!''

Joe struggled with his grin, but soon his shoulders began shaking with laughter. He stood up and came around the table.

"You're laughing at me," she said, her lips quivering in pain. "You think I'm crazy for coming over here with these lame ideas. But they aren't lame, Joe. I just want you to think about what you're doing."

"I haven't thought about anything else in a long time," he whispered, the laughter still in his voice. "And I'm not laughing at you. I'm laughing because it makes me feel so good that you care enough to come up with these...these cockamamy excuses why I can't get married."

"I'm not saying don't get married," she corrected quickly. "I just mean not to her."

"Who?" he asked, still grinning. "You don't even know who we're talking about. For all you know she could be the most perfect choice in the world for me."

"But she's not!" she cried. "She comes from the dating equivalent of junk mail! She's anything but perfect!"

"She's not," he added, "because she's not you? Is that it?"

"What? I wasn't in the running. I didn't want..."

Joe's smile danced in his eyes. "You're jealous again," he said. "It's written all over you."

"I am not! I told you, I came here out of friendship."

"Friendship is usually a little more logical. Jealousy, on the other hand, doesn't care about logic. And you, my little angel, don't have a logical bone in your body at the moment."

She stepped back, livid. "Your ego never stops amazing me! I came over here trying to help you, and you...you..."

"If you really want to help me, Brit, do something about it," he challenged. "If you're so upset about me marrying a junk mail bride, then stop me. You can, you know. If anyone has the power to change this, you do."

Brit stood paralyzed as he narrowed the distance between them and pulled her into his arms. His kiss was gentle, beseeching, offering. She felt tears burning her eyes again. *Oh God,* she prayed. *Please don't let him see me cry.* She held the tears at bay as the kiss deepened, and she felt her heart melting and dripping like poison into her veins. Why was he doing this to her? she asked herself. Why was he stripping her soul bare and piercing it again and again? Didn't he understand? Didn't he realize that she was in love with him?

In love with him!

The idea shocked through her like an electric current, and she jerked out of his arms. It wasn't true. It couldn't be.

"What is it?" he asked.

She pointed at him, wavering on her feet as though she would faint. Tears welled more threateningly in her eyes, and her mouth quivered like a child's.

"That . . . that kiss. That ought to tell you something right there! It . . . it should tell you that you're by no means ready to get married!"

"Not true," Joe whispered. "It tells me that I just about can't wait another day. I might just have to elope."

The barrier of her lashes broke, and hot tears traveled down her face. "Then I feel sorry for your wife!" she shouted. "If you can kiss me like that and then go marry someone else . . ."

Joe's breath caught at the tears streaming down her face. He reached for her hand. "Oh, babe, I never meant to make you cry. I'm sorry—"

"Don't touch me," she cried, shaking him off. "And don't apologize. Just think about it. Can you really marry someone else after—"

"No," he cut in distinctly. "No." The game was over. The stakes were high, and the sight of Brit's tears made the outcome more crucial. But he had won. They had both won. "I can't marry someone else. I can't."

When he pulled her back into his arms, she seemed small, defenseless, wrung out. He kissed her with soul-scourging fierceness, with determination that was stronger than her denial, with intent too powerful to fight.

Had she won? she wondered as she basked in his adoration. Had she really talked him out of it? Had he really said that he couldn't marry anyone else? Or had he even intended to in the first place?

She broke the kiss and gazed up at him, her liquid blue eyes breaking his heart. "Did...did you say that you couldn't marry anyone?"

"No one other than you," he whispered.

Her eyes rounded as clarity dawned.

"I love you, Brit," he said, gazing into her eyes with entreaty that couldn't be denied. "And the whole country is waiting for you to say yes, so that I can set their curiosity to rest and end their stupid contests and settle their bets." He sighed and wiped her moist cheeks with the tips of his fingers. A few leftover sobs escaped her throat, making her seem even smaller. "And I want more than anything to get on with my life...with you...."

A wad of cotton rose to clog Brit's throat. It couldn't be her...couldn't be. "But...but what about your search? All those letters? All those women?"

"What can I say?" he asked with a shrug. "Custom mail-ordered goods are usually damaged before delivery. I found that out with the brownies."

"And you see *me* as a sure thing?"

His smile faded, and a fragile look of uncertainty replaced it. "Hardly. You're the least sure thing I've ever had. But you've taught me that it isn't *anyone* I want, but *someone*. Someone I want to spend my life with. The woman I love."

The words stopped her heart and rendered her lungs functionless. His eyes were eloquent with emotion long held inside and honesty that he'd had to contain for fear of chasing her away. His hand came up to touch a strand of her hair sticking to her wet cheek, and he wove it through his fingers, then brought it to his lips. "I love your hair," he whispered in a husky voice. He watched her lips, slightly parted and quivering, and brushed the damp strand across them. "I love your lips."

Her eyes drifted shut, and he leaned down and pressed a soft kiss on each eyelid, making a sigh drift from her lips. "I love your eyes," he said.

His hand trailed to her neck, and she swallowed. He dipped his head and nuzzled her throat. "I love your neck," he breathed.

Her heart thudded, and she knew he could feel it in the pulse point against his lips. Moist and hot against her skin, he moved upward to the shell of her ear. He bit lightly, making her shudder. "I love your ears."

When his mouth brushed hers, she held her breath, waiting to lose herself in him. But he pulled back, swept her expression with his eyes while his hand roamed through her silky hair. His lips touched hers again, then retreated, and she wanted to cry out in frustration.

"I'm gonna marry you, Brit," he whispered. "You know that, don't you?"

Before she could answer, his lips touched hers again, his tongue making a painfully slow entrance. She felt herself slipping, surrendering, loving the man she held in a way that she had vowed never to love anyone. Her hands slid through his hair, thick as night, and she realized she needed him as well. But that couldn't be. Brit Alexander had never needed anyone.

I'm gonna marry you, Brit. His kiss continued to admonish, to plead, and she felt for a moment as if he wouldn't let her go until she said yes. Her heart wanted to shout it. Yes, yes! But reality intruded like a blaring light, shaking her of dreams that couldn't come true and fantasies that were wasted efforts.

"Another compromise?" she whispered. "To keep from having to answer your mail?"

He chuckled against her lips. "No compromise. Do you want me to give up the search or not?"

"Of course I do," she whispered. "But not badly enough to commit to you myself."

He let her go and stepped back, the warmth suddenly gone from his face. A chill blew over her. "Come on, Brit. Eight thousand women can compete for me, but I'm not good enough for you?"

"It isn't a question of being good enough, Joe. We've been all through this."

Joe raised his right hand in a mock vow. "I promise not to saddle you with two-point-five kids and a station wagon. We'll have six kids and a Porsche."

"Six kids!" Brit choked. "We'd have to get a bigger house!"

"Is that it? The house? No problem, then. We'll move."

"No, I love this house. We don't have to...I mean..." She snatched her thoughts back and focused them again. "Joe, I'm not marrying you!"

"Oh, yes, you are."

"I'm not! And if you care for me you won't go on with this. I love my career. I love the idea of my own show. Please give this up. Don't take everything away from me!''

The desperate plea jarred him, and he frowned and went to the little black book beside his phone. "Wouldn't dream of it," he said finally. "Hmmm, let's see. Wonder if Kitty likes Porsches."

"Joe, you're acting like a child!"

"*I* am? You're the one who wouldn't admit what you *really* wanted if it jammed a ring on your finger. You don't want that show, Brit. You wouldn't have let me kiss you in the restaurant lobby the other night or in your classroom if you'd cared more for your show. And you wouldn't have stormed over here in the night, knowing that at least twenty reporters are probably staking out this house to see who comes and goes."

Brit gasped. "Oh, good Lord. I didn't think—"

"That's my point, Brit. You didn't think. You felt. You risked everything and came here strictly on feelings. It was the hint I wanted from you, Brit. Just the sign I needed. Now I'm risking everything to go with my feelings. I love you, Brit. And, by God, I'm going to marry you."

Brit let out a defeated groan. "Okay, so my emotions have been a little out of hand lately. So I'm attracted to you. So the idea of you with another woman turns me into a stuttering idiot." She shook her finger at him, her eyes a little too wild. "You can bully me into kissing you, Joe Dillon, and you can bully me into admitting that I want you. You can even bully me into acting like a lunatic. But you will never bully me into marrying you. I won't be bullied into that."

"Then what do you want?" he shouted with frustration. "To never see me again? Talk about bullying. You're the one who made me fall in love with you when my plans were all laid out. There's a price for that, Brit, and you're going to pay it!"

"Why? Why does it have to be marriage? Haven't you ever heard of dating? We could see each other. Date a little. No strings attached."

"Secretly?" he asked with a weak smile.

"Maybe just at first. Till the publicity died down."

He shook his head. "Forget it, babe. It's all or nothing for me. I know what I want."

"And I know what *I* want!" she returned. She shook her head wildly, snatched up her purse. "You're a crazy person," she shouted, starting for the door. "I would *never* marry a crazy person!"

Joe followed her to the door, grinning as if she'd just agreed to the six kids. With gentlemanly finesse, he opened the door and pressed a kiss on her mouth. She jerked away.

"Be nice to me," he chuckled, "and I might let you set the date."

Brit gave a loud, furious groan and fled to her car as fast as she could.

Joe stood at the door laughing until she skidded out of sight.

Chapter Nine

When Brit was nine, she'd had a crush on a boy named William who hid a frog in her milk carton at lunch and caused her to shriek and turn over a glass of water, a bowl of potato soup and a container of chocolate pudding. She had sworn she hated him, but as she did, there was a secret inner smile in her heart that congratulated herself on getting his attention. He must like her or he would never torture her so mercilessly.

The feeling she had toward Joe that night was not entirely different. She hated him for doing this to her, for cornering her and making her feel foolish, for being so sure of himself that none of her objections amounted to dust blown in the wind. But in some deep traitorous corridor of her heart where honesty and emotion reigned, she couldn't help smiling. He had picked her out of eight thousand women, and he flatly refused to take no for an answer!

It was absurd. It was infuriating. But somehow, it was a tiny bit gratifying, and she couldn't deny the little thrill rising inside her, though she knew she would have to deal with this soon. She couldn't feel this way when she had no intention of marrying him. Somehow she would convince him that she wouldn't be swayed.

Not even when he held her in his arms and kissed her like some shadowed figure from the depths of her most romantic dreams, sending her pulse careering and making her breath seem like a thin substitute for air. Not even when he told her he loved her...

She hauled her thoughts back and forced herself to look objectively in the bathroom mirror. Who was she? Was she a woman who could have all her values and principles turned upside down by a smooth-talking hunk? Was she just like Lana Bell, only better at hiding it?

She lifted her chin and gave her face a critical analysis. She saw an attractive woman, full of purpose and intent, a woman who knew what she wanted and had the special talent to make others know what they wanted, too. She was strong and independent, and she enjoyed her times alone and didn't yearn for constant companionship. She enjoyed her routines, her quiet and her predictability.

So what was going on? Why did she suddenly feel as if she had some sort of decision to make? Hadn't she already made it? After all, her career was bound to last longer than a marriage to an impetuous man who saw things in his own peculiar colors and didn't give a hang what anyone thought about his visions.

Sleep finally came late that night, but when she dreamed, it was not of independence or career or the millions of single women she could reach through television. That night she dreamed of six sons that looked like Joe Dillon and the frustrating dilemma over fitting them all into a Porsche!

Brit avoided Joe for the next few days as she would have a contaminated nuclear plant. Her phone rang often from the time she got home until far into the early hours of the morning, but she didn't answer. He knocked on her door repeatedly, but she held her breath and pretended not to be home. He showed up at her next seminar, but the guard she had posted outside it refused to let him in without a registration card, which he could no longer obtain since this class was full.

She stopped reading the newspaper after she saw that he had postponed the long-awaited announcement, and she refused to turn on her television for fear she'd see him leading the reporters further in this charade, or that he would have given hints that would enable them to guess that he'd chosen her. She stayed in her room at night, researching and organizing her test show, which was scheduled to be shot the following week. The more deeply she became absorbed in her subject, the surer she became that she was doing the right thing. Joe would get tired of pursuing her anytime now and give up. She would deal with where he went from here when it happened.

But Brit forgot one thing as she drifted through her life with her blinders on. She forgot the extent of Joe Dillon's determination and his certainty that she was the one for him. So on Wednesday morning, when she bounced down to the parking lot and got into her car, glancing up at the billboard she was growing used to confronting, she couldn't help the scream that escaped her throat.

Joe had changed the billboard, and instead of "Uncle Joe Wants *You*," it now read, "Marry me, Brit."

"All the time! All the money!" Mr. Halbrook raved that morning at the station. "I should have trusted my gut instincts. I should have known!"

"Mr. Halbrook, it isn't the way it seems," Brit pleaded, leaning over his desk. "I never said I would marry him."

"But the publicity! The very idea that he's abandoned his search and chosen you is just too much. How do you expect me to sink thousands of dollars into a television show about single women when the hostess of the show is being courted by the most famous bachelor alive today?"

"I'll tell him to stop," she said frantically. "I'll make him go on television and explain that I never wanted to marry him, that it was all a hoax or something. They don't know it's me. It could be another Brit."

Halbrook jerked the newspaper off his desk. "Says right here in black and white: 'Brit Alexander, popular women's advocate.' How many women's advocates do you know named Brit Alexander? The next thing you know, he'll have your face carved next to Robert E. Lee's on Stone Mountain!"

Brit peered at the paper through narrowed eyes and squeaked, "Oh, my God. I'll kill him."

"I don't want you to kill him. I want you to *stop* him!"

Her eyes flashed back to the man rising from his desk. "Short of marrying him, Mr. Halbrook, I don't know how. What would you like me to do?"

"That's your problem," he shouted, "but just be aware that if something doesn't change in the next three days, that show is never going to be shot. I can find better things to waste my money on. To the women who view this show, it will look like you stood patiently in line with those thousands of other women to be his wife. Investing in you to give single women advice on independence is like investing in Nell Carter to give advice on weight loss. It's a lost cause."

"Mr. Halbrook, I told you I'd sign the contract! I'm giving you what you want!"

"Three days, or there won't *be* a contract!" he bellowed, then left her sitting alone in his office.

It was as if he were waiting for her when she reached his house. Joe Dillon sat idly on the front porch of his log cabin, hands clasped over his stomach, feet propped lazily on the railing around his porch. "I thought you'd never get here," he called before she'd gotten out of her car.

Brit slammed the door with no regard for the window it threatened to shatter. "You..." she ranted, coming toward him with a fire-red face and a shaking finger pointed at him like a .38. "You are certifiable. You're dangerous."

"If you marry me, you can have me committed," he offered with a smile.

"How could you do such a thing to me? How could you ruin my life this way?"

He stood up, his smile fading slightly for the first time since she'd come. "Ruined your life? How?"

"The billboards, the radio ads, the newspaper articles, the television commercials, the spots on national news, the graffiti on the sides of buildings!"

"Oh, those."

"I hate you, Joe Dillon!" she screamed.

"I know, babe, but I warned you. One hint, I said. You know, we're really going to have to set a date soon. You wouldn't believe how these people are breathing down my back."

"Look at me!" she shouted from his yard. "Read my lips. I wouldn't marry you if we were the last two people on earth. I wouldn't marry you if it would cure cancer! I wouldn't marry you if a thousand Russian soldiers had me at gunpoint!"

He leaned over the rail and propped his chin on his hand. "How about sex? Would you marry me for that?"

"You are the lowest, most...most..."

"Despicable," he provided.

"Most despicable human being I have ever known. You know what I think?"

He thought for a moment. "That despite my manipulative temperament, you can't think of anyone more exciting or more lovable or more sincere to spend the rest of your life with?"

"No!" she screamed. "I think that you've hated me from the first moment we met on that stupid stage at Georgia Tech! I think that all this is just to prove that you could charge into my life and ruin my credibility. You told me once that if I were your type you'd charm me in ten seconds flat! Is that the challenge, Joe? Just to see if you can catch the one who doesn't want to be caught?"

Joe's temper flared, and the vein at his temple began to throb as he stood up, rigid. "Give me a break! You think I *meant* to fall in love with you and screw up all my plans? You think I wanted to put my ego on the line and go after a woman who was dead set on turning me down, for all the world to see?"

"Yes!" she said. "I think you're like one of those guys with a death wish who jumps out of airplanes and dodges cars on the freeway. Only you like to do it with women. You want to see just how far you can push them before they attempt murder. Is that what happened with Diana? Did she try to kill you?"

Color drained from Joe's face, and she was instantly sorry she'd mentioned the name. "How did you know about Diana?" he asked, his voice as harsh as she'd ever heard it.

"Jerome told me," she said, crossing her arms and stepping tentatively closer. "He was explaining how you met, and how you had to rush away from the wedding in his flower van."

Joe braced his hands on the porch rail and looked down at the ground. "Jerome has a big mouth," he said without inflection. "And you have a vivid imagination. Diana was nothing like you."

"Then what happened, Joe? If you wanted a wife so badly, couldn't you have taken her? There she was, all dressed up with no place to go. Why didn't you marry *her*?"

"Because she would have made me miserable!" he shouted. He slammed his hand against a log post, then came down from the porch to face Brit. "She was shallow and fickle and a social climber, and she loved my money more than she loved me. You would have hated her."

"But you must have loved her enough to marry her."

"I thought I did," he said. "But I woke up just in time." He raked both hands through his hair, leaving it tousled, then dropped his hands to his sides. "She was a blonde," he whispered, "and hadn't finished college, and came from parents who equated marriage to a roll in the hay...as long as there was money involved." He looked fully at Brit, confession in his moist eyes. "When I decided to find a wife another, safer way, I guess I was looking for an exact opposite of Diana. But then I found you."

The sadness in his tone brought tears to Brit's eyes, but she stepped back, closer to her car, closer inside herself. "Tell me something, Joe," she said, her voice cracking. "If I had never come along, and you'd gone on with this search, you would have been able to fall for any number of other women, wouldn't you? It could have been anybody."

"No," he whispered. "It couldn't have been. I found out something important. I found out that I can't let my computer help me fall in love. I can't use statistics and references to find a wife. I can't line them up and choose like I would a new car. When it happens, it happens."

"Then why won't you *let* it happen?" she asked as the tears threatened to shatter. "Why can't you let it happen to me, without making sure that everything else in my life is destroyed, and I have nowhere else to turn?"

He shrugged and twisted his mouth. "Because I love you," he said, "and I can't stand the thought of your choosing that damned career over me."

She held his eyes for a fragment of eternity, wondering why choices couldn't be simple anymore. "It isn't your choice," she said. "And the harder you back me into a corner, the harder I'll fight."

Joe sat down on the front steps of his porch and traced the wood grain with his finger. "What did Halbrook do?"

"What do you think he did? He threatened to pull the show if you didn't stop this rumor immediately. He won't even give me a chance if something doesn't change. I've worked for this all my life, Joe, and now I'm not even going to get the chance because of you. If you really do care for me, how can you do that to me?"

"Easy," he said, looking up at her without the slightest trace of guilt. "The same way you tried to undermine and degrade every possibility I had for a wife. You saw me making a mistake, and you tried to stop me. If you take this show, you'll be locked into being single for the rest of your life. You'll have to wear it like a nun's habit, and you'll never get rid of it. The deeper you get into it, the harder it'll be to cast it off."

She slapped at the tears running down her face. "But that's something I'll have to work out for myself, Joe. You can't do it for me."

Joe propped his elbows on his knees, rubbed his face viciously. "All right, babe," he said at length in a voice that was barely audible. "I'll call off the dogs and disappear for a while. You tape your show, and give it your best shot. And when it comes to making your choice, just remember that I can give you dimensions more than the adoration of your fans or the achievement of your talent. I can give you love."

"Love doesn't always last that long," she whispered.

"Yeah, well," he said, "neither does my patience."

And before she could formulate a reply, he had gone into the house and closed the door behind him.

* * *

The morning sun washed through the windows of the modest Dillon estate in Birmingham—brightening the home where Joe had grown up and learned about family love. Quietly he stepped through the front door and strolled to his father's study, the place that emanated his father's personality and gave Joe a sense of wanting to continue the process of success and family. His father had found both those things and discovered the special balance between them that made him adored by his children, his wife and everyone who knew him.

He turned back to the foyer and looked up the stairs, and thought how this house had been chaotic this time of morning when he was a kid. Boys running up and down the stairs in mad dashes for their rides to school, his mother barking off orders and reminders and admonitions, his father yelling for his tie or his pair of blue socks. A faint smile played across Joe's lips, then died as he recalled how difficult it was to obtain that peculiar bit of happiness. It wasn't like his company, where he'd worked day and night until it had reached the goals he'd set for it. It wasn't like his finances, where he'd been able to plan and study and invest until he had more than he'd ever dreamed of. It was different. And no matter how he'd tried, no amount of computer bytes or late hours or statistical data could help him to duplicate the family he'd grown up with. It just couldn't be done.

Sighing defeatedly, he shuffled toward the back of his house. "Mom? You home?"

He heard something drop, and his tiny pepper-haired mother scurried from the back of the elaborate house, arms spread wide. "Joey! What are you doing here? Give me a hug." She threw her arms around him, then yanked him down and boxed his ears, her joyous expression fading into a scowl. "You stupid, stupid boy. You're here to smooth out your ruffled feathers, aren't you? That's what you get for making a spectacle of yourself! What's her name? I want to congratulate her."

"Mom..."

"Don't 'Mom' me, Joseph Dillon," she said, dragging him toward the kitchen as she went on. "You've always gone at things with a vengeance, but this wife thing took the cake. You deserve whatever abuse she's given you. Is it that Brit girl I've been hearing about?"

"She won't marry me," he said.

"And it's no wonder. I wouldn't have married you, either, you big baboon. Marriage isn't like business. You can't run it like one. Boy, do you have a lot to learn."

Joe leaned against the kitchen counter and crossed his arms as he peered down at his mother. "You know, Mom, she's a lot like you. Maybe that's why I chose her."

"Well, if she's like me, she must have given you a good swift kick in your pants and sent you on your way. You're not the easiest person to tolerate, young man."

"Are you mad at me, too? Have I embarrassed you?" he asked, knowing before he did that the question would send his mother reeling.

"*Embarrassed* me? Was I embarrassed when you got arrested for parachuting off the Peachtree Plaza Hotel building? Was I embarrassed when you had your picture on the front page of the *Constitution* for breaking a new record for bass fishing with a fish that you'd bought at a trophy shop?"

Joe tried to control his smile. "Guess I never have been real easy."

"Want to know what the girls in my garden club said about this wife-hunt?"

Joe snickered and reached into the cookie jar for the cookie that always seemed to be there, despite the fact that none of the children still lived at home. "Not really."

"Well, you're going to hear it, anyway. Agatha Sams told me that *her* Robert didn't have any trouble finding a wife, and that he married before he was twenty-three. I replied, politely of course, that we all understood how he had to take the first one who came along."

Joe bit into the cookie, surveying his mother with laughing eyes.

"Geraldine Colemon said she thought it was a publicity stunt, that no one in their right mind would ever really conduct a search like this. I informed her that my Joey had *never* been accused of being in his right mind."

Joe chuckled and pulled a chair out at the table.

"And then there was Faylyn Seals." His mother sighed dolefully.

"Pretty bad, huh?"

"Terrible," his mother deadpanned. "She sent in her application."

Joe's eyes widened. "The old lady with the fantastic brownies? I remember her." He chuckled. "I think she made it to the top twenty."

"I might have known," his mother acknowledged with a doubtful grin. "We think she might be getting senile, but what can we do? Anyway, in answer to your question, no, I am not embarrassed. But I have been waiting for you to come here with your tail between your legs. No son of mine would pick a wimp for a wife, and I knew that any decent woman you chose would put you in your place after your ridiculous shenanigans."

Joe looked down at the cookie. Suddenly he was no longer interested in it. "All I wanted was a wife, Mom. A family, like you and Dad had. Is that so wrong?"

"As usual, Joey, your intentions are good. Your methods, however, are criminal."

Before he could protest, his mother had handed him another cookie and insisted upon cooking him a decent breakfast, since she blamed malnutrition for his inability to think straight.

Joe was anything but pampered for the next four days. He spent most of his time on the back acres of the estate, chopping wood that the family wouldn't need for months. The grueling work was good ther-

apy, he thought, but it didn't help him to forget the
woman from whom he was running.

Dumped! Wouldn't the guys in his college frater-
nity have gotten a laugh out of that? Ol' love-'em-and-
leave-'em Joe Dillon, campus stud, who went through
women like he did breath mints. But he wasn't a college Casanova anymore. He was forty years old, successful—and lonely as hell. And he was in love with a
little vixen who would murder him if it wasn't illegal.
Damn! How could he have been so stupid as to start
the whole mess with this wife search? It had seemed
like such a good idea, such a calculated way to get
what he wanted. It had always worked before. He'd
done it with new inventions, with products he'd
wanted to sell, with the top executives in his company. It had always paid off before.

And then Brit Alexander had come along and shot
the barrel off his pistol. Talk about fate!

He whacked the ax into the log, his muscles rippling with the effort. She had compared herself to
Diana, when she had no idea how different she was.
Diana had been the type he had believed he should
marry. The perfect executive-wife type. A little too
perfect, in fact. It was then he'd discovered that he had
to pick a wife that *he* could cuddle up to, not one his
business associates could. One who entertained him
and their children more than she did his customers.
Diana was a social butterfly, hungry for money and
the power it brought with it, too caught up in her ul-
timate goals to see the beauty happening on the way.

But he couldn't blame her now. He wasn't all that different. Wasn't that what had driven Brit away in the first place? That he was too caught up in getting to matrimony to enjoy just getting to know her?

But damn it all to heck, he wanted to marry her!

The sound of the log splitting beneath his strength sounded like justice in a world where there was so little.

Things hadn't really changed that much since he'd left home, Joe thought that night after dinner, when his dad lay back in his recliner, watching a rerun of his favorite old show, "The Waltons," while his mother bustled around in the kitchen. Joe had seen the episode a dozen times, and each time it left him awed and lonesome. He propped his feet on the coffee table and crossed his hands over his stomach.

"Wonder what happened to John-Boy when he grew up," he mumbled absently.

"He became a writer," his dad drawled. "He's the guy who narrates at the beginning and end. Doesn't sound like his voice to me, though, does it to you?"

Joe smiled. "No, I mean about marriage. Did he get married to a girl just like his mother and have a houseful of little John-Boys-and-Girls, or did he have the miserable misfortune to fall in love with a suffragette girl rallying for women's right to vote?"

Arnold Dillon had never been one to tolerate self-pity, and he wasn't about to start now. "The problem with you," he said gruffly, "is that you have to have everything your own way. You wind up cutting off your nose to spite your face.''

"What is that supposed to mean?" Joe asked irritably. "You've sat here with me for four nights and never brought up the subject of my marriage, and now you come up with a line like that?"

"You're a smart man," his father said. "You figure it out."

And that night as Joe lay in the bedroom where he'd kept his collections of turtles, baseball cards and birds' nests when he was a boy, Joe did just that. What he decided was that he wanted Brit on any terms he could get her. She had a dream that she considered more important than his. If he wanted her—all of her—he'd have to let her achieve her dream. Marriage and family would have to wait. First he'd make her fall in love.

Chapter Ten

It was a crime that the sun shone so brightly in the early spring sky when Brit felt like a hailstone in a storm, hurtling as fast as she could toward an impact that would shatter her.

Miserably, she sat at the intersection of that parking lot she had come to hate and gazed up at the billboard Joe had had painted white. No longer did his face smile down at her. No longer did it demand her hand in marriage.

She revved her engine, then sat with it idling for a moment as she stared off into space. Where was he? It had been four days and she hadn't heard from him. Last night, in a fit of insanity, she had even called his house. There had been no answer.

What did she expect? she asked herself. She had made her position clear the last time she'd seen him. She'd left him with no choice, and he'd reminded her that his patience was running out. Had it run out completely?

She pulled into the line of traffic, then headed for the television station. She had managed to convince Halbrook to go ahead with the test show, since Joe seemed to have dropped out of sight and pulled his ads and billboards. They were shooting today, and the contract would be ready for her to sign if all went well. Finally, her dream was coming true. Ironically, she couldn't have been more miserable.

Where was he? The question rang out in her heart, colliding with the fear that it was too late for her, that he'd given up and changed his mind. She was better off, wasn't she? This high-wire act called love was not for her. She needed stability. Accomplishment. Something she could build herself—to be proud of when it flourished and take the blame for if it failed.

Like marriage, that tiny voice in the back of her mind taunted. What bigger accomplishment was there these days than to build a happy marriage and a thriving family?

She screeched her thoughts to a halt and reminded herself how many women she'd be reaching through her show. Miserable women, victimized women, lonely women, women on the verge of being everything they could be...

She took the ramp off the interstate leading to the television station and wondered if she was really doing it for all those women, or for some sort of self-gratification. Was Joe right about her locking herself into a new kind of prison? Would this popularity cover her like a nun's habit that she couldn't cast off?

"No," she said aloud, wondering why tears were springing to her eyes on what should be the most exciting day of her life. "I want this show. It's right for me. I've worked for it. I've earned it."

She pulled into the station parking lot, where soon she would have her own parking space in one of the select areas, along with her own elaborate dressing room and office. It was all in her contract, but somehow she wondered if she'd traded her freedom for a wardrobe allowance and a nameplate on her door.

Slumping over the steering wheel, she settled her eyes on the studio's red brick. If she lost the show, if it bombed, if the ratings never got out of the zero percentile, what would she do? Try again later? Go back to the seminars that were fulfilling in themselves? Continue her lecture tour?

And what if she lost Joe, because of his all-or-nothing attitude and her give-in-and-do-it-my-way mentality? There wouldn't be any chance of trying at love again. She wouldn't have the heart. Would her life ever be as satisfying as it had been, now that she had found that special something that made her sparkle? Could she go on as if she'd never met him?

When weighed, the effects seemed uneven. If she lost the show, she could go on. If she lost Joe, she couldn't. But if she chose Joe, she would lose the show and everything else.

Wiping her eyes with shaking fingers, she went into the studio. Eugenia was waiting in the makeshift dressing room Brit was using until they decided whether or not she was to be a permanent fixture.

"Thank God you're here," Eugenia drawled in her jaded eastern accent. "For a minute there I was afraid that man had changed your mind and that you were riding off into the sunset with him."

For the first time, Brit didn't come back with a scathing denial. The idea wasn't entirely unappealing. Brit went to the mirror and began redoing her lipstick. "I haven't heard from him. He must have left town."

"Well, he does have some mercy, after all," Eugenia sighed. She slapped a file down in front of Brit and leaned on the makeup table. "I've got all your notes here that we went over, and the staff has already lined up about twenty callers to get us off to a great start. By the way, darling, your hair looks fabulous. We're going to be millionaires!"

Brit gave her agent a vacant look, then, as if dazed, settled her eyes back on the mirror, staring unseeing at the woman reflected there.

"Uh-oh," Eugenia said. "You're in a mood."

"I'm fine."

"No, you're not fine. You're gloomy, and I really have to warn you that Halbrook will sense it a mile away. Get rid of it, Brit, or that contract won't be waiting for you to sign when we finish taping."

Brit sat in the dressing room for a while after Eugenia left her and tried not to think of Joe or that contract or the inevitable sacrifices that one choice or the other would demand of her. Finally, telling herself she had wasted enough time, she forced herself to go into the studio, where quite a bit of money had already been spent on the bright, elaborate set that resembled a multicolored living room, filled with greenery just as she'd ordered. The lights were already blazing hot, and cameramen and technicians scurried around readying the set for the important taping.

Halbrook stepped over some cords and came to meet her, his cigarette clamped between his lips. "Those callers are raring to go, Brit. And everything's all set. We're ready anytime you are. Remember, this is a test. The real show will be live, so we're going to shoot it straight through in one take, just to make sure you can handle the pressure." He grabbed the cigarette out of his mouth and exhaled a long stream of smoke. "Don't let me down. We may have a small budget, but a lot of money's already been spent on this."

Brit nodded blandly and took her place on the couch. Through the blaring lights, she saw Eugenia assessing her critically.

"Isn't she a little pale?" Eugenia asked Halbrook.

"She's fine," Halbrook spouted. "Let's get on with this."

Brit forced a bright smile and reminded herself that this was the culmination of everything she'd wanted in her life, as the director shouted "Action!" and the theme music began to play.

Then the announcer's voice came clear and upbeat over the speakers. "Welcome to *Single and Loving It*, starring America's foremost expert on living the single life, Brit Alexander!"

Although she launched into her well-prepared script with the gusto she'd had weeks ago, before she'd ever met Joe Dillon or knew the impact of those choices she promoted, Brit felt a sick, smothering feeling rising inside her. And she wasn't at all certain that she could pull this off, after all.

She'd made it through forty-five minutes of the show, answering questions posed by the callers, when a particularly distraught woman's call came through. "Brit, I'm Sheree from Charleston, South Carolina."

"Hi, Sheree," Brit said. "What's your question?"

"Well, I've been divorced for about a year and a half now, and I've been a big follower of yours and done everything you advised. See, one of the problems in my marriage was that my husband didn't want me to reach any measure of independence. I sort of felt trapped."

"Not unusual," Brit commented.

"Well, now I've gotten established in a career I really like, and I live alone, and I have a whole new circle of friends. I've proven to myself that I don't have to lean on a man."

"Sounds like you're doing fine. What's the problem?"

The woman hesitated for a moment. "Well, the problem is that I still love my husband. As much as you'll probably hate me for saying this, I'd drop my career and my independence in a minute if I thought he'd take me back. Am I crazy?''

Brit felt a lump rising to her throat, blocking out her speech. Dead air passed as she groped for an answer. A month ago she would have told the woman that the relationship was not healthy if she felt she had to be totally absorbed in it, that it hadn't worked once and probably wouldn't again, that giving up her career for a man was, indeed, crazy. But today she wanted to cry, and tell the woman to drop everything and run back to him as fast as she could if she felt that strongly about him.

In a wobbly, feeble voice, she heard herself saying, "Sheree, sometimes we're faced with difficult choices. And when it's all or nothing, we have to weigh which one we can live more easily without. Single life can be a good life. But it isn't the only life. I hope that isn't the message that I'm getting across to you."

"You're gonna marry him, aren't you?" the woman asked suddenly. "That Joe Dillon guy."

The director began slicing his index finger across his throat in a frantic effort to cut the woman off, but Brit ignored him. With a soul-rending sigh, she looked into the camera, knowing the show would never be aired now, and whispered, "God help me, I guess I am."

"Home, Jerome," Joe said when he stepped into the front seat of the limousine at the airport.

"Yo, Joe. So how was the trip? D'ya set a date for the wedding?"

Joe slumped in the front seat and rested his head on the back. "There isn't going to be a wedding," Joe said. "I've decided to take it slow and easy. Court her a little. Drive her crazy."

"Sure you still remember how?"

"Hey, I wasn't so bad in my prime. I just got bummed out. Never had anyone I wanted to impress so much."

"Seems sorta strange, not thinkin' about the wedding," Jerome said. "You know, Lana Bell—that's Brit's red-haired friend—she seems to think you ought to just throw Brit into an airplane and take her to the south of France where she can't speak the language to scream for help, and just show her what's good for her."

Joe chuckled at the picture, but somehow there was no mirth in his heart. "The lady already knows what's good for her. And it isn't me."

"Hey-oh, this ain't the Joe who got on that plane before. You hit your head or somethin'?"

"My mother hit it a couple of times," Joe admitted. "Guess she and my ol' man knocked some sense into me."

Jerome shook his head and watched the road as he drove. "So you really want to go home? Not to her hotel? Don't even wanna tell her you're back?"

As much as the thought tempted him, Joe shook his head and gazed out the window. "No, let's give her a little more breathing room. She's trying to get her show set up. I don't want to get in the way."

* * *

"All right, Lana Bell," Brit shouted into the phone that afternoon. "Where is he?"

"Where is who?"

"Joe Dillon. I know you've been seeing Jerome. He must have told you where he is."

"Oh, him." She could hear the smile in Lana Bell's voice, and she wanted to throttle her. "Why would you be interested?"

"Where is he!" she screamed.

"He's home," Lana Bell said, laughing. "Right here in Atlanta."

"No, he isn't. I've called for days."

"He got home this afternoon. Jerome was picking him up today. He's been in Birmingham visiting his parents."

"Home?" The quiver in her voice was too obvious, but she didn't care. She had nothing more to lose. "You mean he's really home?"

"He really is."

Her heart fell. "Then why didn't he call? Why didn't he come by?"

"Maybe he's come to terms with your rejection. Frankly, I thought by now he would have taken my advice and tried the south of France scenario, but since he didn't, I guess he's decided to wing it alone."

"I don't know what you're talking about, Lana Bell," Brit said quickly. "But thanks. I have to go."

With that, she hung up the phone and rushed down to her car.

* * *

Jerome was on Joe's front lawn when Brit drove up, but he didn't hear her because of the headphones he wore. Off-key, he sang along with an old Temptations' song, dancing to the rhythm as he polished the limo.

Brit got out of her car, straightened the big shirt that hung out over her jeans and tapped on Jerome's shoulder. He jumped.

"Fo' the love of God, woman, don't ever sneak up on a man like that. You could get killed." He took off the headphones and surveyed her as if seeing her for the first time. "Sure didn't expect to see you here. Neither did Joe."

"Is he here?" she asked anxiously.

"He's here," Jerome said. "But he's asleep on the couch. Guy's beat, like he hasn't slept in days."

"Can I go in?" she asked. "I won't wake him."

"Have at it." Jerome glanced at the door, then uncertainly back at her. Finally, he lifted his ample shoulders. "Just do me a favor and don't get him all worked up if he does wake up. He's a good guy. He tries to do the right thing."

"I promise," she whispered, then, smiling, tiptoed into the house.

Just as Jerome had warned, Joe was asleep on the sofa, wearing nothing but a pair of faded jeans. His arms were clasped behind his head, his biceps contracted, and a slight sunburn coated his shoulders, then blended into a tan down his chest.

Brit felt a burst of rightness as she knelt beside him, admiring the thick chest with the heavy sprinkles of dark hair compelling her fingers to touch him. But she wasn't ready yet. There was too much she had to do before he woke. Smiling, she pressed a light kiss onto his hair that smelled of forest breeze and whispered, "I love you, Joe."

Then she left him and went to the kitchen to prepare for the moment he woke.

The sweet, warm scent of brownies drifted through the air, making Joe stir. Slowly, he opened his eyes, sat up halfway and cursed under his breath. He could have sworn he'd thrown all those brownies away. Had Jerome saved those, too? Or was he baking up a fresh batch?

He dropped his feet to the floor and rubbed his eyes. Damn, he hadn't meant to fall asleep. Through the window he could see that night had fallen, and he hadn't gone through his mail or checked in with the office or returned any calls....

He stood up and stretched, then froze in mid-motion when he heard a man's voice rattling off perfect French. Then, suddenly, he heard a woman's voice in the kitchen, in a less than perfect accent, repeating the words. A befuddled frown stole over his forehead.

Quickly, he started toward the kitchen, but stopped cold when he saw a manila envelope taped over the doorway. He jerked it down and pulled out the contents. Oh, God, he moaned silently. One of them had gotten in. Some woman was waiting for him in the kitchen, when he couldn't feel less like meeting anyone. He scowled down at the new application, then grudgingly at the black-and-white glossy of the brunette with the prettiest face he'd ever seen. Brit's face!

A loud laugh rolled out of his throat, and he threw down the application and picture and dashed to the kitchen. The sight he encountered there made him fall against the doorway, laughing until his eyes were full of tears.

Brit was standing at the oven, mimicking the French on the cassette he'd given her, but her hair was all brown and curly, and there were chocolate smudges on her cheek and fingerprints on her jeans. She heard him laughing and turned around. *"Bon soir, Monsieur Dillon,"* she muttered in a sexy voice. *"Comment allez-vous?"*

He stumbled toward her and took her in his arms. "Oh, my God," he chortled. "What did you do to your hair?"

"It's a, how-you-say, *vig*," she informed him, still murdering the French accent. "You vanted a brunette; you got a brunette."

"No," he said, pulling her against him. "I wanted a blonde. Where's my blonde?" He pulled off the wig and sighed when her blond locks tumbled out over her shoulders. The wig fell to the floor as he wadded the locks in his hands. His lips met hers, and she tasted of brownies and commitment and love.

"Did you find my application?" she whispered against his lips.

"Mmm-hmmm," he said. "It wasn't necessary, you know."

"Not necessary? You said once that you couldn't consider me seriously until I submitted my application. I even tried to get you a mold of my teeth, but I couldn't get a dentist's appointment in time."

He pulled back to look at her, unable to grasp what this meant. "Why?" he asked.

All humor drained from her eyes and a fragile solemnity filled them. "Because," she whispered shyly against his lips. *"Je t'adore."*

"In English," he returned breathlessly. "I don't have time to look that up."

"I love you," she said again.

He closed his eyes and leaned back against the wall, crushing her against him as his mouth ravished hers. He wanted to stop time and hold on forever—to demand that they find a justice of the peace in the next five minutes—to beg her to move her things into his home. But he'd come too far to ruin things now. "No demands," he breathed. "No commitments. We'll take it nice and easy. No strings attached."

"The heck we will," she objected. "You don't think I did all this for a *date*, do you? For heaven's sake, I even got my parents back together...almost. If it works out, I'll meet all of your requirements by the time we're married."

"Married?" he asked, stricken. "But what about your show? What about your seminars? I would have taken you on your own terms, Brit. You were right about it being your choice. I had no right—"

"I made the choice," she whispered. "There isn't going to be a show. Just a marriage."

This time when she kissed him, she touched his chest as she had longed to do since the night in her hotel room. She slid her fingertips across his nipples, reveling in the feeling of control when he shivered and moaned. His hand came up under her sweater to the soft mound of breast straining for his touch. "Where's Jerome?" he whispered.

"I sent him home," she said. "We're alone."

"Good." He flipped her around until she was against the wall, and slid his other hand under her shirt. She moaned at the gentle touch as his mouth breathed life into her.

A burning smell broke their kiss, and Brit cast a worried glance at the stove. "Uh-oh. I burnt the brownies."

"That's all right," he whispered. "I'm tired of brownies."

"But I burnt them. What if I'm not housewife material, Joe? What if I just can't cut it?"

"Then we'll have to find you a new job," he whispered. "You could come up with a new show for all women instead of single women...."

"Or I could write that book about your search for a wife. You did keep all the stuff for me, didn't you?"

"You'll have to fight it away from Jerome," he chuckled. "But it's all intact. It's sure to be a bestseller."

"Written by the woman who won," she whispered.

Joe picked her up in his arms and nuzzled her neck as she arched her head back. "Come here," he said, taking her from the kitchen. "I think it's about time you saw my bedroom."

"Are you happy, Joe?" she whispered as he carried her through the house. "As happy as I am?"

"Well, I don't know," he teased. "There's just one thing that disappoints me."

"Really?" she asked, stricken.

"Yeah," he said. "You gave me the eight-by-ten glossy, the application, the brownies...but I didn't see a pair of your panties anywhere."

Brit buried her face in his neck and chuckled lightly. "Oh, you're going to get them," she assured. "Any minute now. But you'll have to take them yourself."

"I think I can handle that," he said as he lowered her to the bed. "By the way, do you still want to spend the honeymoon in a padded cell?"

"Do you think we can get reservations with such short notice," she asked, giggling.

"No problem," he rumbled. "They've been holding one for me since I met you."

Brit's clear laughter died in his kiss, for there were more serious matters to attend to.

*   *   *   *   *

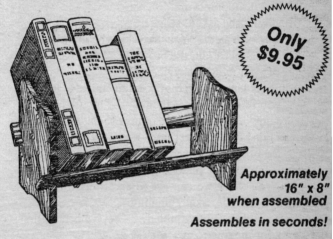

Silhouette ❀ Romance

COMING NEXT MONTH

AVAILABLE THIS MONTH:

Silhouette Romance™

Legendary Lovers Trilogy

BY DEBBIE MACOMBER....

ONCE UPON A TIME, in a land not so far away, there lived a girl, Debbie Macomber, who grew up dreaming of castles, white knights and princes on fiery steeds. Her family was an ordinary one with a mother and father and one wicked brother, who sold copies of her diary to all the boys in her junior high class.

One day, when Debbie was only nineteen, a handsome electrician drove by in a shiny black convertible. Now Debbie knew a prince when she saw one, and before long they lived in a two-bedroom cottage surrounded by a white picket fence.

As often happens when a damsel fair meets her prince charming, children followed, and soon the two-bedroom cottage became a four-bedroom castle. The kingdom flourished and prospered, and between soccer games and car pools, ballet classes and clarinet lessons, Debbie thought about love and enchantment and the magic of romance.

One day Debbie said, "What this country needs is a good fairy tale." She remembered how well her diary had sold and she dreamed again of castles, white knights and princes on fiery steeds. And so the stories of Cinderella, Beauty and the Beast, and Snow White were reborn....

Look for Debbie Macomber's *Legendary Lovers* trilogy from Silhouette Romance: *Cindy and the Prince* (January, 1988); *Some Kind of Wonderful* (March, 1988); *Almost Paradise* (May, 1988). Don't miss them!

SRT-1